SHE
THAT ...
STAN ... HER . . .

Inside the stark white living room, she circled him, backing him across the room toward the couch. He dodged her and moved over to the windows, stared out at the gray winter sea.

"Adragon?"

"Yeah?"

"Turn around."

He wanted to say *No!* He wanted to bolt, run out of the apartment, out of the building, out of her life. He wanted her more than he wanted his next breath. He was afraid of her.

"There are no such things as vampires, are there?" He turned, almost against his will, and asked again when she didn't answer immediately. "Are there, Del?"

She was standing in a shaft of light that fell from a tall lamp in the far corner of the room. Her robe lay in a green puddle at her feet.

"Are you afraid of vampires, Adragon?" she asked in a faraway voice. "Are you afraid of me?"

"I just don't know why you want to pretend to be a vampire."

"I don't pretend, Adragon. That's what I am. . . ."

SWEET BLOOD

PAT GRAVERSEN

ZEBRA BOOKS
KENSINGTON PUBLISHING CORP.

*This book is dedicated to my sons,
Jon and Paul Erik, who believe
in the reincarnation of love.*

ZEBRA BOOKS

are published by

Kensington Publishing Corp.
475 Park Avenue South
New York, NY 10016

First printing: September, 1992

Printed in the United States of America

I wish to thank Charlotte Simsen and The Quincey P. Morris Dracula Society for their invaluable inspiration in the creation of this book and its characters.

Life is real, life is earnest,
And the grave is not its goal;
Dust thou art, to dust returnest
Was not spoken of the soul.

Longfellow

Chapter One

Adragon stirred the blood with the tiny gold spoon. The sharp smell set his teeth on edge, and he wondered how it would taste. In two or three minutes, he would know. He filled the spoon and moved it to his left, to the lips of a middle-aged woman who was perfectly ordinary, except for the maniacal gleam in her eye, and the bat jewelry that adorned her wattled neck.

She swallowed the red liquid, and Adragon placed the crystal dish in her hands so that she could offer it to the person on her left. There were thirteen members of the Society of Vampires in the room, plus their two guests, and the dish circulated quickly.

When it was Elsbeth's turn to partake, she rolled her eyes and feigned thirst, then satisfaction, acting as if she were a not-too-bright character in one of her books.

"Careful, Mother," Adragon murmured under his breath, "they might get dangerous if they thought you were making fun of them."

She turned to him and drained the last of the blood into the spoon. It looked black in the dim, candle-lit room, and it had thickened in its trip around the circle but Adragon knew that he had to accept the proffered spoon and its unholy benefaction. He was the last in the circle, and everyone else had partaken without a single sign of revulsion among them. Anyway, it was totally cool: he had just turned seventeen, it was exactly three minutes after midnight on All Hallows' Eve, and he was sharing blood with vampires.

Chapter Two

But it wasn't really blood, was it? They walked through the parking lot of the restaurant where the Society of Vampires had held its meeting, Elsbeth's tiny hand curled around Adragon's arm.

"What was in the little crystal dish, Mother?" Adragon asked as soon as they were far enough away from the others.

"Blood, darling," Elsbeth answered in the same tone she would use to say that it had been a lovely evening.

He said, "Sure," but he knew it wasn't, although the exact composition of the potion eluded him.

He concentrated on driving his mother's Jag, handling the powerful car expertly. She chattered all the way, unleashing the energy built up over the course of the past two hours.

"My God, was that weird or what?" she had asked as soon as they were in the car with the doors closed and locked against vampires and other creatures of the night. "Do you think they're really vampires? Well, they sure as hell seem to take themselves seriously. That ceremony!" She paused to take a short, necessary breath. "They want me to write a book about them, you know. They want to be 'understood.' That's why they invited us tonight, to impress me. They want me to tell the world that they exist, without revealing any of their secrets. Why me?" she sighed, and fell into silence as he turned onto the street that ran parallel to the beach.

"It's beautiful, isn't it?" she asked, meaning the house, and Adragon agreed that it was. He made it a practice never to disagree with his mother, unless he seriously wanted to make a point.

He pleaded a headache and closed his door on the hum of Elsbeth's old IBM Selectric. She wrote her books on the state of the art computer that took up an entire wall of her office, but she brainstormed on the old typewriter on which she had written her first book, almost ten years ago. Sometimes Adragon watched her work when she was struggling with a new premise, agonizing over the best way to pull together into a cohesive whole all the elements of a tale that she alone could tell. He would sit quietly in a corner of her large office, by one of the tall windows that provided a view of the Atlantic, his feet tucked under him in a comfortable chair. He would hold a book open on his lap but they both knew that he wouldn't read it. He would watch her face, so like his own, and marvel at her intensity, her singularity of purpose, as she created a world and peopled it with characters more real than the humans who walked the beach beyond their house.

Tonight Adragon had things other than Elsbeth's creativity on his mind. Vampires. Were they or weren't they? He went over the entire evening in his mind, starting with the moment he gave the coded knock and grinned foolishly at the eye peering out at him through the peephole. He was asked, quite seriously, to give the secret password and, as soon as he did so, the door swung open.

Elsbeth clung to his arm as they were admitted to a dark den lit only by candles and a blazing wood fire. If he hadn't been enjoying himself so much, he might have been frightened, as Elsbeth pretended to be. A boy close to his own age dressed all in black greeted them, if you could call it a greeting. He bowed in their direction and waited silently for Adragon to introduce himself and Elsbeth, although he obviously knew who they were, or he wouldn't have opened the door to them. It was a game, and Adragon didn't like games but Elsbeth squeezed his arm and he knew that he would have to play along.

"I'm Adragon Hart and this is my mother, Elsbeth." The boy leaned past Adragon and paid homage to his mother. "Mrs. Hart, welcome. It is an honor to have you here amongst us. Let me introduce you to our little group."

He led them into the middle of the small, very warm room, and raised his hands to get the attention of the dozen or so people sitting in groups of two or three just outside the circle of light cast by the fire.

"People, this is our special guest of honor, Elsbeth Hart, the famous horror writer with whose works you are all familiar. Mrs. Hart, we welcome you to the Society of Vampires."

"I'm very happy to be here," Elsbeth answered in the enchanting voice that captivated her audiences and made her a much sought after speaker. "I realize that you don't usually invite guests to your meetings, and I'm honored that you've chosen to make an exception for me. The young man with me" — she turned to him and smiled engagingly — "is my son, Adragon, who is equally grateful for your kind invitation."

There was a polite smattering of applause as Elsbeth stepped into the shadows and followed the young man's long blond hair to a bar where drinks were being served by members of the Society. Obviously, even waiters and bartenders were barred from the room when the vampires were in attendance. Adragon felt Elsbeth's breath tickle his ear before he heard her whisper: "Tough crowd tonight, kid." He bent his head to convince her that she had charmed them speechless. When he raised his eyes, he looked into a pair of huge, luminous green eyes, as mesmerizing as the sea.

"Hello," he said, and his voice caught his mother's attention and brought a look of distrust to her face. Or was it a look of disgust? With Elsbeth, he was never quite sure, in spite of the gossips who swore that mother and son could read each other's minds. He always heard the gossip, although he usually pretended to be above listening to it.

They go to the same hairdresser . . . their clothes are always color-coordinated . . . they go everywhere together . . . he's never out of her sight . . . he anticipates her every request . . . some people say . . . doesn't it make you wonder?

He didn't let the things people said bother him. His mother was a famous woman, and a rich woman, and the truth was that he hadn't yet found another female who was half as interesting. Of course, he was only seventeen, and he had never before seen a girl as beautiful as the one who stood behind the bar preparing Perrier with lime twists for him and his mother.

Elsbeth accepted her drink with a polite "Thank you," and dragged Adragon toward the fireplace where she held court until the ceremony began. It had been a fascinating evening, one more unforgettable experience shared with his mother, who attracted interesting people the way honey attracts bees.

Deciding to leave the house, Adragon traded his jacket and tie for a hand-knit sweater Elsbeth had purchased for him on a trip to Ireland to promote the publication of her eighth novel, which was set in Dublin. He went out through the back door, crossed the deck, and climbed down the steep wooden steps to the beach.

14

He walked along the edge of the water, kicking at the sand. Adragon never tired of looking at the sea, or of knowing that the beach on which he stood belonged to his mother, and would one day belong to him. Unhappier times were always just out of reach of his conscious mind, days when he stood on the crowded public beach at Asbury Park and begged his mother to stay another half hour, when he knew that it might be weeks before they could afford to return.

After walking several hundred feet down the shore, he turned to retrace his steps. A figure glided out of the shadows in front of him, and Adragon's heart hammered in his chest. The shadow form was long and thin, and it trailed a flowing cape in its wake. A breeze off the ocean lifted its wings and carried it toward him. It was ugly and beautiful in its horror, and its mouth opened to call out to him, "Adragon . . ."

He laughed with relief and hoped that he hadn't given away the terror that had nearly crushed his chest. It was only Raymond, who owned the house next door. The "cape" was an old jacket thrown over his shoulders against the chill of the night, and the "wings" were the jacket sleeves lifting on the stiff breeze that blew in from the ocean.

"How was your evening?" the man asked, and Adragon found that he couldn't answer until he had swallowed the hard lump in his throat.

"Very interesting," he managed after a bad moment. "Raymond, you wouldn't believe these people. But I can't tell you; we were sworn to secrecy. If we divulge their secrets, they'll bite us on the neck."

Raymond laughed appreciatively and glanced up at the house.

"She's working," Adragon answered the unspoken question.

"A new idea?"

"How did you know?"

"Your mother's a morning person; she only works at night when she's excited about a fresh concept."

"She was inspired by the vampire people."

"Did they adore her?"

"Doesn't everyone?"

"Don't be so angry about it; she doesn't love anyone but you." Raymond laughed and slapped him on the shoulder. "It's getting colder; better get inside before I catch a chill."

They walked toward the house together and Raymond left him at the steps.

"Tell your mother I asked after her."

"Sure."

Raymond was a retired surgeon, a widower who lived alone in the huge beachfront home he had shared with his wife. He had no offspring, no known relatives, and few friends for a successful, attractive man. Adragon suspected that the doctor stayed on in his gloomy mansion because he was in love with Elsbeth.

He watched from the deck as Raymond climbed the steps to his own house before he went inside. He pulled the sweater off over his head and tossed it on a chair, then fell across his bed, put his hands behind his head, and stared out the window at the night sky. There were so many things he needed to think about; too bad old Raymond had interrupted his solitary walk on the beach.

Adragon closed his eyes and saw again the closed door, heard the coded knock, saw the door swing open with the use of the magic password. He had felt foolish as hell, close to giggling like a little kid while he followed the secret rituals. The blood (was it really blood?) had tasted bitter but it hadn't been as bad as he'd imagined it would be. He swallowed it and a strange sensation came over him, as if he was really a vampire . . . as if this first

16

taste of blood was only the beginning, the birth of something he was meant to be.

Then before he knew it, he and Elsbeth were out in the parking lot, walking toward the Jag, and he had forgotten the strange foreboding (yes, that was the word!) feeling that had come over him when he tasted the blood.

One more thing to think about: the beautiful girl with the green eyes and the long strawberry-blond hair. He hadn't dared look at her with Elsbeth standing so close to him, no more than a stolen glance or two. But when he did dare to let his eyes sweep over her, she smiled at him and they became coconspirators. He wondered if he would ever see her again, and decided that it wasn't very likely.

It was late when Adragon got up to brush his teeth and relieve himself in his private bathroom. He padded around in the dark, changed into a T-shirt and a pair of pajama bottoms, and turned down his bed. Before he climbed in, he cracked the door an inch and listened for the sound of his mother's typewriter. After a moment of silence, he heard it, and he smiled indulgently. "You're a piece of work, Elsbeth," he muttered, and threw her a kiss which she would acknowledge when she saw him tomorrow.

He was up early, out on the sand for a run before the sun burned off the morning mist. Then home for a tall glass of milk and two English muffins with peanut butter and jelly, his favorite breakfast when Elsbeth was too busy to insist that he stick to his "exchanges." He took the food to his room and watched *Good Morning America* while he ate; he admitted to being a Joan Lunden freak.

He came out of his room when he heard Elsbeth banging around in the kitchen and caught the smell of Folgers wafting through the house. He had done his homework, and had plenty of time for a cup of coffee with his mother before he left for his afternoon class.

Most of his friends thought it was weird that he was attending Brookdale Community College on a part-time basis when Elsbeth could afford to send him to Harvard or Yale, but Brookdale was what he wanted to do, and Elsbeth went along with it. She didn't have a college degree, just a nursing certificate, and she often talked about going back to school. Still, she didn't mind giving her son a little time to ease into his future slowly instead of rushing into it headlong.

"Hi, Mom." She was sitting in the breakfast nook reading *The New York Times*. When she wasn't writing, she was reading; he was used to it. He leaned to kiss her cheek and she turned away from him, so that his lips brushed her hair.

"Keep your distance," she warned, "I look terrible without my makeup."

"You're beautiful."

"And you're prejudiced."

"Not me. My mother raised me to be an impartial judge of beauty."

"So she did." She looked up at him over the rim of her reading glasses. "I neglected you last night, love. Did you take your insulin? How was your glucose level this morning?"

"I'm fine, Mother. I went for a walk on the beach last night. Raymond sends his regards."

"Dear Raymond. We'll have him over for dinner as soon as I finish my synopsis."

"Are you excited about it?" If she wasn't, it was a waste of time, and she would be impossible to live with when she made that discovery.

"Oh, Adragon, it's the best one yet."

"You always say that."

"I always mean it."

Every day of the next week followed the same routine.

18

Adragon went to school; Elsbeth went to her office to work. She broke around six and they went out to dinner at some little place nearby where they were known well enough to be served quickly and efficiently. When they got back to the house, she went straight to her office, where she usually stayed until after midnight. Adragon amused himself with a video or a book, and ended his day as he had started it, by running or walking on the beach.

Their schedule changed subtly ten days later when Elsbeth finished her synopsis and moved to the computer to start chapter one. Now she worked from early morning to late afternoon, cooked dinner for herself and Adragon, and retired early, leaving her son to entertain himself. Sometimes he went out with a friend from school, but there wasn't much to do for recreation once Seaside shut down for the winter. In the summertime, the guys found someone with a car and cruised up and down the main drag until the local cops chased them away. When they found some willing girls, they'd spring for pizza on the boardwalk or a game of miniature golf. Some nights they'd get lucky, and the girls would let them drive down to a deserted stretch of beach, park the car, and spread a blanket on the sand. The Jersey Shore was a great place for a guy to live in July and August, but it was a boring place to be stuck when the boardwalks closed up for the winter.

Late one evening near the end of November the telephone rang, breaking the habitual silence of the house. Adragon snatched it up before it rang a second time and disturbed Elsbeth.

"Hi, this is Del. Del Keelan? I met you on Halloween, remember?"

"Of course, I remember." Delphine, the girl with the

19

green eyes; how could she think he might forget?

"Are you doing anything?" she asked as casually as if they were the same age, as if she was the kind of girl he could call back and ask the same kind of question.

"Now?" he asked stupidly. "Uhh . . . nothing really. Watching the news on TV." But she wasn't calling for him; he had never considered himself to be an especially lucky person, and that would be like winning the lottery. "Listen, Elsbeth is into her work schedule now; I couldn't possibly disturb her this time of night. I'm sorry."

She hesitated just long enough for him to notice before she said, "I wasn't calling Elsbeth; I called to talk to you."

"Well . . ." He wanted to shout Hoorah! or say something incredibly ridiculously childish that would probably make her hang up on him. She was the sexiest girl . . . no, the sexiest *woman* he had ever seen, and she scared him half to death.

"How about going for a drive? Can you sneak out? It's way past eleven."

"I don't have to sneak out," he knowingly played right into her hands, and made no excuses to himself for doing it. "Elsbeth's my mother, not my keeper." Not my lover. Not my other half.

"I'll meet you on Route 36, on the corner of the street that runs nearest to your house."

"How do you know where I live? Why do you—"

She had hung up, and Adragon hurried to grab a jacket and walk as casually as he dared to the corner she had named. Just as he reached Route 36, the main road that ran through the town from north to south, a red Nissan pulled up to the curb just a foot in front of him. She lowered the window and leaned out, her hair dark reddish-blond in the dim light, her eyes more vibrantly green than he remembered.

20

"Jump in," she said, smiling at him, warming him from the inside out. She was wearing jeans and a green sweater that matched her eyes, and she didn't look a day over twenty, although his mother had told him that she was "quite a bit" older.

He climbed into the car, banging his knee, feeling clumsy and too young; he would have traded the next ten years of his life to be twenty right that minute.

Chapter Three

Adragon fastened his seat belt and settled back, mortified by his awkward assault on the girl's car. She seemed to be completely oblivious of his discomfort. She drove like a maniac down the coast, slowing as they came to the seaside towns of Asbury Park, Ocean Grove, Avon by the Sea, Spring Lake, Sea Girt. The smaller towns were dark and quiet, waiting for the winter to pass, dreaming of their return to glory.

In Point Pleasant, she pulled to the end of a street that ran right up to the beach, killed the headlights, and turned to face him. It was too warm in the car, and she was too much woman for Adragon. They were too close, the atmosphere too intimate. He knew how to talk to girls his own age, because he felt superior to them. After all, he was Elsbeth Hart's son, famous by osmosis, sure to be famous in his own right soon enough. But this woman was different.

He flushed when she asked him if he was too warm, and floundered when she tried to draw him into conversation, but within ten minutes he was relaxed enough to be telling her his life story. His and Elsbeth's, which were entwined. She wanted to know what it was like to be dirt-poor one day and filthy rich the next. She had been born with money; now she owned her own shop. She had no frame of reference.

She was curious about his relationship with his mother.

"Does she let you have girlfriends?" Del asked teasingly.

"Elsbeth doesn't tell me what to do. We're two adults who just happen to live together. She treats me as an equal." He was angry. The girl might be drop-dead gorgeous, but she sounded too much like the people he overheard talking at the required cocktail parties and autograph signings he attended as his mother's escort.

"Hey, don't be angry with me." She surprised him by running her fingers through the tight curls at his temple, and brushing his ear with a long fingernail. When he jerked away from her, she smiled knowingly.

On the way back to Elsbeth's house, Del surprised him again.

"They're going to ask her to join the Society."

"Who? You mean Elsbeth?" He glanced at the girl's profile as she nodded and wondered why she looked so serious. It was all in fun, wasn't it?

"Are you a member?" he asked.

"You saw me at the meeting."

"I know, but I hoped you weren't —" He didn't know how to continue, and he covered his blunder with a phony cough that didn't fool the girl for a minute.

"Get serious, will you? You knew I was a member when you saw me serving drinks. You might not know much about us, but you must know that we couldn't allow a bartender to overhear our conversations or observe our rituals."

"But you allowed me."

"Only because Elsbeth's acceptance of our offer of membership was already guaranteed."

"That's impossible; who could guarantee it?"

"That's something I really can't tell you, so don't ask me

23

again, okay? I shouldn't have told you anything."

"Do you take turns serving drinks?"

She flashed him a quick smile. "About once a year the privilege is mine."

"I can't picture Elsbeth playing bartender."

"They'll brainwash her into thinking it's an honor, trust me."

She pulled the Nissan over to the curb in almost the same spot where she had picked him up light years earlier. "Don't tell her, Adragon. I shouldn't have told you, but I wanted you to know that they were going to ask her."

He watched the little red car speed away, drowning in waves of disappointment. She had called him not because she wanted to see him but because she felt the need to warn him that his mother was going to join the Society of Vampires. He was painfully aware that she hadn't mentioned anything about his being asked to join. And why should he be asked; he was a nobody. Elsbeth was the rich and famous one, the one the Society wanted, the one everybody wanted. If she joined, it would be the first important thing she had ever done without him.

"I'm not her little boy," he whispered to the disappearing taillights of Del's car. "I don't need her anymore.

"And if she thinks I'll forgive her for joining without me, she's crazy," he yelled aloud, as he rounded the corner and headed straight for the beach for his evening run.

The night air calmed him, and carried his anger away. He made a firm decision that he would say nothing to Elsbeth about the Society until she brought it up. *If* she brought it up.

When he came in from his run, Elsbeth was waiting on the deck.

"Where were you?" she asked, not treating him as an equal. She was wearing old pajama pants with an over-sized T-shirt, and she looked ten years younger than her actual age. Her hair was tousled, giving her a little girl look that angered Adragon and made him resent her demanding tone of voice.

"One of the guys from school picked me up; we went down to Pizza Hut." He spat out the information, letting her know how he felt about the question.

She leaned close to him, testing his breath for the garlic powder he loved to sprinkle generously on every slice.

"I didn't eat," he improvised. "I didn't have any bread exchanges left."

"Then why did you go, to torture yourself?"

"I went along for the ride, okay? For the company. To hear the sound of a human voice that isn't electronically reproduced."

"Oh, love, I'm sorry." Her body sagged, and the superior attitude slid off her face. "I've never been able to balance the two sides of my life, and I always end up neglecting you, the most important person in the world."

"It's all right, Mom, really."

"I'm going to change, Adragon, I promise you."

"I love you just the way you are."

"Do you? Do you really?"

"Yes, I do, but I'm beat, Mom. I'm gonna go to bed now."

"Good night, sweetheart."

She kissed him near the lips, and he thought of Del Keelan's lips.

" 'Night," he answered. He wanted to get away from her, to think about the girl, to remember the feel of her fingers on his ear, in his hair.

He spent the next week in solitude, except for the two hours a day he sat in the classroom at Brookdale, the professor's words flowing over his head without penetrating his brain. He relived every minute he had spent in Del Keelan's presence, and agonized over his lack of sophistication.

He dreamed every night but his dreams were not of the

25

beautiful redhead. His night visions were of vampires who looked surprisingly like ordinary people. They stood in a circle in a dark room, firelight reflected in their eyes, and passed a crystal cup of blood.

The last week in November, Adragon and Elsbeth drove to the Ford dealership in Brielle to accept delivery of his birthday gift from her: a new white Ford Mustang convertible with all the options, which Adragon had picked out three weeks before. Choosing the car had been one of the high points of his life. Walking into the showroom, climbing in and out of the shiny new display models, choosing the color he preferred. When the salesman, only a few years older than Adragon, started to fill out the order forms, he had cleared his throat and discreetly mentioned that it would be necessary for Elsbeth to obtain financing for the car in her name, since Adragon was just seventeen. God, it was so cool. "We'll be paying cash on delivery," he'd answered casually, and the young salesman's face had registered relief that he was assured the commission on the sale, and the painful knowledge that he was dealing with a person several years younger than himself who could probably buy and sell him. It was a given that the guy couldn't have afforded to drive a new car himself if a demo wasn't included in his job perks.

Now, on the ten minute drive to the dealership, Elsbeth handled the Jag with finesse. She loved powerful cars and she loved driving, but sometimes she got in a "nondriving" mood. Then someone else (Adragon since he turned seventeen) would be drafted to chauffeur her around for days or weeks, until her mood changed again.

"They asked you to join, didn't they?" Adragon suddenly blurted out, not knowing that he would ask the question until it was too late to stop it from crossing his

26

lips. Elsbeth was quiet and withdrawn today, and her mood dampened his. Before his surprise question, he had been wondering why people tended to remember only the good about a given situation. When Elsbeth was between books, he couldn't wait for her to conceive her next idea. He looked forward to watching her: her smooth brow, her blue eyes that could change from light to dark without warning, her tousled dark curls. He loved the way she concentrated with every part of her being on the words she would use to fill reams of white computer paper. To Adragon, Elsbeth's acts of creation were far more exciting than the spine-tingling horror novels which were the final results of her creativity.

But between books he always forgot her moodiness: her long periods of silence, her demands for quiet in the house when she was working, her withdrawal into a world where her characters were more important to her than her son.

Well, the question was out there; she would answer it in good time. Finally, she turned to face him and he took his frustration out on her.

"Keep your eyes on the road, Elsbeth," he advised, and she clenched the steering wheel until the skin over her knuckles was translucent, proof that he was getting to her.

"What do you want from me, Adragon?" she asked, spitting the words out, as if they were little arrows laced with venom, carefully aimed.

I want your attention; I want to be as important to you as the characters you create. What he said was: "They asked you to join the Society of Vampires, didn't they?"

"Yes, they invited me to join."

"And?"

"And I haven't made up my mind yet. You know how I feel about joining clubs and organizations. They all want to use me to attract attention to themselves. They want to be listed as one of my 'affiliations' on my bios."

"Is that what the Society of Vampires wants from you?"

"Who knows what they want? I already told you that they want me to write a book about them."

"Is that what you're working on now?" She was superstitious; she never shared her ideas with him, only her enthusiasm and her finished projects.

"For God's sake, Adragon, stop acting like a jealous little boy. I haven't even decided to join the stupid vampires."

"The way I heard it, they were sure of you before they invited us to their meeting."

"That's ridiculous." She was nervous, jittery, holding something back. Adragon was furious.

"Forget it, Mother, I can see you don't feel like talking." She had pulled into the dealer's lot, and he got out of the Jag and slammed the door hard, knowing that she hated that. Then he strode into the showroom, leaving her to follow behind him, another thing she hated.

As they sat on cushioned chairs in the sales manager's office waiting for the car to be brought around, Adragon ignored his mother and pretended not to hear her several attempts at conversation. He spent his time wondering what the macho types lounging around the showroom thought of him and Elsbeth. A woman in her late thirties and a kid just out of school, both dressed in blue jeans, SAVE THE EARTH T-shirts, leather bomber jackets, and dark glasses. Both with the same curly, shoulder length hair, hers touched up to match his natural color exactly. Were they taken for eccentric millionaires, or did everyone think they were just plain crazy? When the salesman dropped the keys to the Mustang in his hand, Adragon decided that it didn't matter to him what they thought, one way or the other.

That night Elsbeth followed him onto the beach and walked beside him until he slowed down to match her pace. When he made his turn to start back, she touched his arm and stopped him.

"I'm sorry for being so secretive," she said, using her "I'm only doing what's best for you" voice. "They did invite me to join, and I'm going to accept their offer. I need more contact with them if I'm going to finish the book."

"Oh." It was all he could think of to say.

"Adragon, they didn't extend you an invitation simply because there's only one opening. I'm sure that sometime in the future —"

"Bullshit! They want you because you're the famous one, famous enough to get them free publicity."

"They don't want publicity —"

"Don't try to con me, Mother, I know you too well."

She took a step backward and stared at him with shock and amusement vying for predominance on her face. "My God, Adragon, you're jealous."

She sounded pleased, and that made him even more angry.

"We've always done things together," he said, unable to help himself.

"We have to do some things alone; I don't go on your dates, do I?"

"Don't be cute; this is different."

"Raymond's house is so dark," she changed the subject skillfully, "we haven't seen him for a while. Do you think he's all right?"

"How should I know; he's your friend." Adragon shrugged to indicate that he couldn't care less, and Elsbeth left him to walk down the beach. Her faded jeans and bulky sweater made her look as if she was much younger, too young to be interested in a man Raymond Sadler's age. She stopped just below their neighbor's huge, dark mansion and let her eyes roam over its gothic facade.

"Come over here, Adragon," she called, and no less angry, he was still obedient to her command.

"Do you hear something?" she asked when he reached

her side, cocking her head and giving the impression of listening intently.

"No," he answered without bothering to listen. He was determined that he wouldn't be taken in by her little games. He was angry and he would stay angry until he was damned good and ready to forgive her.

Elsbeth gave him a dirty look and he concentrated for a minute. "It's his stereo."

"It sounds like the sea on a stormy day, like rushing water, or —" Or the beating of wings, Adragon thought.

"It's probably one of those new-age recordings."

Elsbeth nodded and let her son guide her back to their own property, but he noticed that she was trembling, in spite of the fact that it was an unusually mild night for the end of November.

"Let's go inside and have a glass of hot cocoa," he suggested. "If you get sick and can't work, I'll never hear the end of it." He was giving her a chance to be the coddled one. He made her a cup of cocoa with miniature marshmallows floating on top, kissed her forehead, and tucked her in bed with wool and down and electric filaments to warm her thin blood. She gazed up at him with adoring eyes and touched his warm cheek with an icy hand, apologizing without words for her frailty, her womanhood. He kissed her fingers and squeezed them before he left her room. It was a part he had played a thousand times before, in a scene that was all too familiar. It was his way of making up to his mother; it was her way of letting him.

Chapter Four

Del Keelan called again on the following Friday night, and although it had only been eight days, it seemed like a lifetime since Adragon had heard her voice. He sadly relayed the fact that his mother was not available to talk.

"What do I have to do to convince you that I don't want to talk to your mother?" The girl laughed, and someplace in the pit of his stomach Adragon felt a stirring that he knew, once out of control, could not be stopped.

"I don't even *know* your mother," Del continued, "and something tells me that we wouldn't hit it off. I'm definitely *not* calling for your mother."

"Why not?" he'd asked stupidly. "I mean, what makes you think you and Elsbeth wouldn't hit it off?" Did he care? It was something to say. In this girl's presence, even separated by miles of telephone line, he was a blubbering idiot.

"Too much competitive spirit, I guess," Del answered after only a moment's thought about the question, then she shied away from the subject, leaving him to wonder what she'd meant by her remark.

"I'm lonely," the girl of his dreams said, and Adragon almost missed this revelation entirely, his mind still on her previous mind bender. "Why don't you come over and keep me company?"

"No," he blurted out.

"You can't come over?" He actually imagined that he heard disappointment in her voice.

"I didn't mean that," he explained quickly, "I meant that you couldn't possibly be lonely. Not you."

She laughed, and he heard bells tinkling in his ear. "Everyone gets lonely sometimes, Adragon. I'm alone by choice; I'm lonely by circumstance. Placing yourself in the middle of a crowd doesn't necessarily make you any less lonely."

"But you're so—"

"Go on."

Say it, Adragon, he urged himself. ". . . so beautiful."

"Thank you." She lowered her voice, as if someone might be eavesdropping. "Come, Adragon. I'll massage your shoulders and ease your tension. Are you tense, little boy? I know a hundred ways to ease your tension."

When he found his voice, he intended to tell her to never call him "little boy" again. Instead, he asked for her address and wrote it down on the back of his English paper that was due tomorrow. School was the farthest thing from his mind, something he did in another lifetime, where girls like Del Keelan didn't exist.

She lived in a condo on the beach in Lavalette. The building appeared to be deserted; probably half of its occupants had either fled to warmer climes or returned to the city to hibernate for the winter. That was fine with Adragon; once he stepped foot in the building, it was as if the two of them were alone in the world. She met him in the lobby and held his hand as the elevator rose to the eighth floor and opened to a short hallway with access to four doors. 8B was ajar; she led Adragon inside and closed the door behind them.

"I'm impressed," he said, taking in the long living room with one wall of windows facing the beach. The room was done completely in white except for several splashes of red: pillows, knickknacks, a telephone, Del herself in something long and flowing, the color of blood.

She left him standing at the window staring out at the ocean while she went to the kitchen for Cokes. Then she seated herself on the white leather couch and patted the cushion next to her.

He was shy suddenly, an awkward boy in the presence of a graceful woman. What in the hell was he doing here? What if she expected him to make a pass? Worse still, what if she didn't? What if she laughed at him? He'd probably end up spilling his Coke on the white carpet.

"For God's sake, Adragon, relax. I won't bite you tonight, I promise."

A vampire joke, just what he needed. "I guess I'm sort of" — he shrugged, and took the hand she held out to him — "sort of out of my element here." Elsbeth's expensive beachfront house was furnished in what they jokingly called "early comfortable," meaning anything that pleased them, anything they wanted, whether it fit or not. No phony decorators for his Elsbeth. He wasn't used to stark white rooms and red-clad girls who made his blood rush.

She handed him a glass, he took a long draft, coughed, and spit Coke down the front of his pale blue sweater.

Del laughed and took the glass from his hand, then patted him on the back until he stopped choking.

"I'm sorry, Del. I hope I didn't get any on the couch."

She indicated that he hadn't, and that it wouldn't have mattered anyway. She leaned toward him and brushed his cheek with her red lips. Gently. A sisterly kiss, although his body didn't react in a brotherly fashion. She eased him back on the couch until he was lying flat, then knelt on the floor beside him. The lights dimmed, and he registered that she held something in her hand, probably a remote control device. A moment later, Bob Marley's soft reggae music filled the room. He wanted to ask if she was into reggae, and tell her that it was his favorite music but he was too tired.

Del had somehow managed to remove both his sweater and his shirt without his knowledge, and she was massaging his neck and shoulders with slim, cool fingers.

"Feel better?" she asked.

"This is great; you really know how to make a guy relax." But talking was an effort; he wanted to lie there with her hands on his body for the rest of his life.

"Umm," she mumbled in answer to something he'd said. "No, don't move, just lie still. Keep your eyes closed."

She lifted his left hand and moved it to her mouth, put her lips to his palm, then traced his life line with her tongue. He tried to grab his hand away but she held onto it tightly.

"Don't do that, okay?"

"Don't you like it?"

"Sure but—"

She draped his sweater across his crotch without releasing his hand. "Now I can't see what's going on down there, so you can relax and enjoy yourself."

Adragon started to protest but she put her finger across his lips to silence him. Then she licked the palm of his hand greedily, and he was glad that she couldn't see what was happening under his sweater. She licked each of his fingers slowly, tickled them with her tongue, then sucked them into her mouth. Her actions were so intensely languorous, so sensual, that Adragon thought he would burst from the tension that was building up in strategic parts of his body. The tingling sensation ran from his fingers to his hand, his arm, his chest, and centered in the bottom of his stomach as she continued.

But underneath his hormones' frantic dance and the liquid desire that coursed through his body, there was something else, something he couldn't identify as easily

34

as the other emotions he was experiencing, some for the first time. He was afraid, scared, leery. His body was totally absorbed with Del but there was a part deep inside his mind that told him to be careful of this woman who had shared blood with him. Did she really think she was a vampire, or was she just fooling around with the Society because she got some kind of a weird kick out of her involvement? Those fleeting feelings lasted only a moment, replaced by the more natural desires of a seventeen-year-old boy.

"Del," he murmured her name and tried to pull her into his arms but she resisted. He felt her draw away and when he opened his eyes, she stood above him, smiling down at him.

"Go home now, Adragon."

"But why — what did I do?"

"You did nothing wrong; there will be other nights." With that enigmatic remark, she left the room, to return with two cups of coffee just as Adragon was pulling his blue sweater over his head.

"When can I see you again?" he asked. The coffee was bitter and he nursed it, watching her face. He had never seen eyes so green, skin so white and flawless.

She shrugged, as if the time they were apart meant nothing, and Adragon's spirits plummeted. Her hands and her mouth had worked to make him forget his place, to forget that he was seventeen and she was twenty-six (or so she'd told him). She'd made him forget that he was ordinary, and she was the most extraordinary creature he had ever seen. He knew without a doubt that meeting her and being this close to her would be one of the serious high points of his life, even if he lived to be a hundred. Being with her lifted him above the ordinary and made him feel that he was special, as she was.

He drove home and sneaked into the house, aware that he was somehow betraying himself (Elsbeth is my

35

mother, not my keeper). The twenty minute drive up the shore with the top down had revitalized him, and given him new hope. She would see him again; she had to. He laughed aloud when he passed a car going in the opposite direction and the other driver looked at him as if he were crazy. Not crazy, he answered the man's superior look. In love. In-fatuation. In-chanted. Crazy, yes. Crazy in love.

Elsbeth didn't come out of her room to accost him, and he went jubilantly to his bed, and willed himself to dream of Delphine Keelan. He did.

His first waking thought the next morning was that he hadn't run on the beach the night before, and his medication would have to be adjusted to deal with a higher sugar level. But that didn't matter; nothing mattered. He was going to live forever; he was in love with Del Keelan.

A week later the telephone rang late on a weekday night, and Adragon realized that he was existing only in anticipation of that sound, living only when he heard her voice or saw her face.

She picked him up on Route 36 and drove faster than before, but this time Adragon didn't bother with the panorama of picturesque towns that flew past the window of the red Nissan. They were only ten minutes from Elsbeth's house when Del swerved off the road and pulled to a stop in front of a beach club that had seen better days.

She jumped out of the car and started running across the sand, with Adragon hot on her trail. She had been silent during the drive, and he was having a hard time gauging her mood. When he finally caught up with her, he was panting but Del was breathing easily.

"What the hell's up, Del?" he asked breathlessly, "what's this all about?"

She looked into his eyes but didn't speak, and Adragon felt decidedly uneasy. Too many people wanted to play games with him lately, and he didn't like it at all.

The night was black, the moon hiding behind thick

dark rain clouds. A fine mist rolled in from the ocean, and it reminded Adragon of standing under a sprinkler in back of the apartment complex when he was six or seven.

"Adragon . . ." Del reached out for him, her arms ghostly pale, and he noticed for the first time how she was dressed. Dark red silky pants that could have been pajamas, with a thin transparent blouse that was already soaked and sticking to her skin. He was wearing sweats, and he was close to freezing.

"Hey, Del, do you want to tell me what's wrong? Did you have a fight with somebody? Why are you dressed that way? It's December!"

She ignored his questions and continued to stare into his eyes with a sad expression. Her own eyes were red-rimmed, teary.

Adragon waited, hoping that she'd decide to return to the car. He was so cold that he felt as if his thing would fall off any second, and if they kept standing where they were, in the shadow of the old cement bath house, cruising cops would probably hassle them.

"Come on, Del, let's go." He took her clammy arm and tried to move her. It worked, in a way. She fell against him and they tumbled to the ground. The sand was heavy, wet, like concrete not quite set. Adragon's left side froze within seconds; his fingers were so cold that they felt nothing when they brushed Del's nearly exposed breasts. But other parts of him felt something, in spite of his discomfort. He was cold, not dead. He rolled over on top of her and she responded by saying his name as it had surely never been said before.

"Adragon . . ."

He tried to kiss her but she pushed his face away and lifted his right hand to her lips.

"Don't tease me, Del, it's too fuckin' cold."

He felt a sharp sting at the end of his finger, the kind of zing he got when he cut himself shaving. He looked down

37

at his hand and saw a single crimson drop, saw her slipping something into her deep pants pocket. A flash of fear raced to all his nerve endings; all thoughts of romance dwindled with his limp member.

He tried to stick his finger in his mouth to ease the pain, the way he had tended his own wounds when he was a child, but he hadn't expected that Del would be so strong. She lifted the damaged finger to her lips and licked the dot of blood from the tip. Her eyes never left Adragon's, and the noises that she made—the sucking, smacking noises—filled the night and eclipsed even the roar of the waves slapping the shore.

"Cut it out, Del." Had his voice quavered? Shit, who cared. She was scaring him and if she didn't stop, he was afraid he'd do something. Slap her or something. Pee in his pants maybe.

"Don't," she murmured around his finger when he tried to pull away from her again. "I need you, Adragon."

"Just stop it, okay? This isn't funny, Del. Now let go of my damned finger."

She stopped, and Adragon retrieved a shriveled, icy digit. He nursed it in his other hand, vainly attempting to bring back the circulation.

"I'm a vampire, Adragon; I thought you knew." *I'm a nurse, Adragon. I'm a flight attendant, Adragon. I thought you knew.*

"That's not funny. Absolutely, positively *not* amusing. If you want to scare the shit out of me, why don't you buy an Usi?"

He stalked away from her, staggering through the sand that sucked at his soaked Reeboks. His heart was beating at about three times its normal speed, thudding in his ears, pounding painfully in his throat. He climbed into the passenger seat, wondering about his chances for a heart attack at the ripe old age of seventeen. Was it possible to be scared to death? To literally die from fright? If it was, he was a prime candidate for early extinction.

Seconds later, Del sat beside him, and Adragon couldn't restrain the gasp that escaped from his mouth. Her complexion was no longer white; it was peaches and cream. There were patches of color high on her cheeks, as if she had applied blush on her way across the sand. Her eyes sparkled, even in the dark interior of the car.

"I'm sorry, Adragon. It wasn't supposed to happen this way, but my need was too great."

"Does Elsbeth know you're doing this?" He was angry, and he didn't care if he sounded like a petulant child threatening to tell his mommy what she'd done.

"Why would I tell Elsbeth that I want to make love to her son?"

"Is that what you call this—this depraved SHIT you do? You call that making love? Well, I've got news for you, babe—"

"I'm sorry, I shouldn't have brought you here. You're frightened, aren't you?"

"Damn straight! A deserted beach, at midnight, in the middle of winter—this isn't exactly my idea of a picnic."

"Oh, Adragon, you're taking this far too seriously. I only wanted to be alone with you." There was something different in her voice, some new quality. Was she laughing at him?

"Why wouldn't I take it seriously?" he shot back.

"Because it's all a game, that's why."

"If it's a game, I'd say you play like a pro."

"I studied acting in college. Do you really think I'm good? Good enough to play a vampire? Did I really have you worried, my sweet Adragon?"

"Oh, shit, you really had me going, and you know it."

His voice broke and she pulled him into her arms. His finger still throbbed with pain and his feet were lumps of ice. But she warmed him with her lips and made him forget his physical misery. When the long, searching kiss was

39

finished, he looked into her eyes and he knew that it was more than just a game. He also knew that he would give Del Keelan anything she asked for, even his blood.

Chapter Five

In the light of day, the events of the preceding night didn't carry the same weight. In fact, they were almost laughable. Almost. Adragon stood before his reflection in the bathroom mirror and chided himself for being so scared, so in awe of Del's declared vampirism. "Jesus H. Christ, what an act!" he told himself, shaking his head to clear it of such foolishness.

He threw himself down on the bed clad only in his undershorts. The winter sun was warm and his smallish room felt overheated this morning. Or was that his warm blood heating up, sending out signals to the vampires? He laughed again, and reached for his psych book.

He couldn't concentrate on the chapter he was supposed to read for his class later in the day. Now that Elsbeth was joining the Society, would she start to think she was a vampire, too? Would she start to behave the way Del had acted last night, stuffing people's fingers in her mouth, trying to suck out their blood drop by drop, gurgling and smacking her lips and literally nauseating everyone she approached? He sure as hell hoped not; he still had a reputation of sorts to maintain.

A picture of his mother's pouty lips parted to show her gleaming little teeth flashed through Adragon's mind, and he doubled over with laughter, tumbling and rolling on the bed. He giggled until all the humor disappeared and only the pain of his exclusion remained.

Unfortunately, it was too late to stop the question from taking root in his brain and tormenting him for the rest of the day: why did they insist that they were vampires? What was the attraction? What satisfaction did they get out of making themselves laughingstocks?

Everyone at the Society meeting he had attended had seemed a little weird; maybe it was a case of mass hysteria on a small scale. Maybe if he did a paper on the Society for psych class, he'd finally catch up with that elusive A-plus he'd been chasing all semester.

He went to school, nodded through his class, and got a C on the pop quiz; he never had gotten around to reading the material.

At home again, he had dinner with Elsbeth: thin slices of marinated beef served with wild rice. His mother was always watchful of his diet. They ate in almost complete silence; she was moody and withdrawn, laying her fork down every several minutes to make notes on a pad beside her plate. "Working at the dinner table?" he asked her once, since that was one indulgence she usually didn't allow herself. But the question didn't make her laugh and lay down her gold-trimmed Mont Blanc. She grunted something he didn't catch and kept at it, while Adragon ate alone.

After dinner, he wandered through the house checking the telephones, making sure that they were in working order. There were four of them in the house, and since Del's first call, they had become the instruments of his torture. He damned them if they rang, damned them if they didn't.

There was a sleek almond-colored phone hanging on the wall just inside the kitchen door, and a fancy gold one in Elsbeth's dressing room. This one usually had its ringer turned off. There was a beige phone/answering machine in the den which carried an electronic reproduction of Adragon's voice: "Hi, this is Adragon Hart . . ."

The phone in his bedroom was brown, square, nononsense, and it was the one he sat and stared at when his tour of the house was finished. Elsbeth had gone back to her room to try and work out a difficult passage in the book, the same one she had been struggling over at the dinner table, so she would not be on the phone. Anyway, she was not a telephone person. She was not her usual chatty self if there was no one to see how she sparkled. She didn't have a telephone in either her bedroom or her office and she left the answering of the phone and the recording of important messages to her son.

Early in the morning, Elsbeth would take a few minutes to make or return important calls; that was the only time of day she chose to use the instrument. Until this particular night, Adragon had always taken Ma Bell and AT&T pretty much for granted. Between dinner and the time the telephone finally rang at 8:45, he both hated it and loved it.

Adragon picked up the receiver on the second ring and held it to his ear. "Adragon?" she asked. He pushed his finger down on the disconnect button and layed the receiver aside. He hung it up again a few minutes later, in case someone else was trying to get through. Then for the rest of the evening he sat beside the phone in his room, waiting for it to ring again, so that he could make the decision all over again, but it kept its silence.

Before he went out for his run, he switched the answering machine on, taking the chance that Elsbeth would hear the message, if Del left one.

He ran north, fast and hard, his knees pumping, his arms pulling him through the dense fog that hid the sight of his beloved ocean from view. He was already tired when he turned to run south, and it was nothing new to have his mind and his eyes play tricks on him when he was

43

tired and his sugar level was high from either exhaustion or stress.

That was why the apparition that appeared before him on the beach barely slowed him down. Her loose, flowing hair and her long diaphanous gown were surely conjured up from the depths of his need to see her, despite his fear of her madness. The ghost figure held out its arms to him but as he drew closer, the apparition drew back, so that he couldn't seem to close the distance between them.

Adragon stopped running in front of his own house and bent over, hands on his thighs, to catch his breath. He contemplated waking Elsbeth to ask if he should increase his insulin dosage, in view of the mirage that had hovered in front of his eyes until just a moment ago when he drew to a standstill.

There was a feather-light touch on his arm, barely felt through his running jacket. He shuddered and looked away into the far distance, seeking the Del-like thing that had lured him across the sand. Soft lips brushed his cheek, and he straightened slowly, fearfully, but she wasn't beside him. She was standing in front of Raymond's house, several hundred feet in front of him, her skirt lifting in the ocean breeze, her hand raised to brush her wet hair from her face.

As he watched, the ghostly figure walked behind the huge Victorian house and disappeared. "She isn't real," he murmured, sure that if he followed her, she would reappear, then disappear again. She was a figment of his imagination, his temptation, his raw desire. Anyway, he didn't want to find her in the shadows of Raymond's mausoleum, in the dark, damp night. She was either crazy or — Either way, she wanted his blood, and he was afraid of her.

He went to his room after locking every door and window and pulling the shades. He stretched out on the bed

44

and pulled his pillow over his head. If she knocked . . . if *it* knocked, he didn't want to hear it.

The next two evenings, Adragon went out with some guys from college who were always trying to include him in their group. But after two nights of mediocre movies followed by hanging out at Friendly's Ice Cream store, devouring huge concoctions that sent his blood sugar level soaring, and flirting with teenyboppers in adjoining booths, Adragon was bored with the world of normal seventeen-year-old boys.

The morning following the second of these outings, he woke up knowing that he would stay home that night, and that he would answer the phone when it rang. And it did ring, at exactly nine o'clock, as if she, too, had been waiting all day, knowing what would happen.

"Adragon?"

"Yeah."

"Where have you been?"

"Nowhere. I mean here. I've been here all day."

"You know what I mean: last night and the night before. Are you still angry?"

"If I was still angry, I wouldn't have answered the phone."

"I need to talk to you."

"So talk," he answered flippantly, then grew apprehensive during the long silence that followed.

"You don't want to forgive me, do you?"

"Hey, Delphine . . . Del, I don't know what you want from me. You're way out of my league and I know it, so it's not as if I'm expecting anything. Don't interrupt me, okay? I might not have the nerve to say this tomorrow, but tonight I do. You're really a gorgeous girl — scratch that, a gorgeous woman. Drop-dead gorgeous. But I'm not a sadist or a masochist and this blood thing—"

"I'm not either, Adragon. If you really want to know what I want from you, have you ever looked in the mirror?

Any woman alive would have fantasies about you, about being close to you."

He laughed to break the spell of her low, hypnotic voice telling him that a woman like her found him desirable. "I look just like my mother," he said, and Del laughed with him.

"Maybe so, but your mother is one hell of a good-looking woman."

"Elsbeth?" He thought about it for a moment, then agreed. "I guess so. Can we talk about something else?" If he became convinced that he was sexy, then he would have to admit that his mother was, too, and even though he often joked with her about looking sexy, it was something he didn't want to consider too seriously.

"Sure," Del answered his question, "we can talk about you forgiving me for scaring you the other night."

"You didn't *scare* me, for Christ's sake. You surprised me, that's all, and it made me mad—angry."

"Are you angry now?"

"No, I'm okay."

"Thank you for forgiving me," she said so seriously that he almost laughed again. "When I couldn't get you on the phone, I thought . . ."

Del talked on in the same vein for several more minutes. Adragon tuned out on the content of her speech, and found himself wondering why she didn't apologize for the vampire act. She was apologizing for scaring him, but not for the actions that had scared him. Or angered him, as the case might be. She finally said good night and hung up, without mentioning when she would call him again, if ever. Later Adragon realized that he had forgotten to ask her if she had been on the beach in front of Raymond's house wearing a long, flowing dress, beckoning to him from the shadows. Then he was glad he hadn't asked; it was a stupid question.

For days Adragon either watched the phone or walked

46

on the beach, half expecting Del to appear out of the mist. This time, he vowed that he would run to her and draw her down beside him in the damp sand. He fantasized about making love to her, and at night he tossed in his bed, as he dreamed about the pain she might inflict on his body. In the dreams, she was a crimson-clad angel of pain, and he welcomed her gifts, knowing that there was no escape from them. Anyway, it was only a game, wasn't it?

While her son moped and daydreamed, Elsbeth worked like a demon on *The Vampire Chronicles*. She was writing about a fictional society which reflected the views of the real Society of Vampires and she was obsessed with her ideas.

Adragon was surprised when she decided to take a break on Sunday evening, cook dinner, and invite their neighbor, Raymond Sadler, to join them. He walked over from his house at 6:30, wearing Dockers, with a tweed jacket over a white turtleneck, dressed for his part as the wealthy retired physician.

"Why don't you marry him?" Adragon asked Elsbeth as they stood at the kitchen window watching Raymond struggle through the sand and climb the steps to their deck.

"Whatever for? Anyway, he's too old for me; you know I prefer beautiful young lovers."

"That's probably because you're young and beautiful, yourself," Adragon answered, knowing his lines only too well. But the truth was that he couldn't remember his mother ever having a lover, although she flirted outrageously with men of all ages of whatever social background.

His father had left them when Adragon was little more than a baby, and Elsbeth had never quite recovered from being deserted. At least, that was what she had intimated one night when she had consumed a little too much wine.

The cool evening air entered the house with Raymond, and Adragon shivered, remembering the strange night he had spent on the beach with Del. She hadn't called back; maybe she had only wanted to be forgiven before she moved on to someone else. Maybe he would never hear from her again.

"Adragon, my boy, I haven't run into you on the beach lately. Don't tell me you've given up running."

"No, I've been there. I guess we're just on different schedules these days."

"No schedule at all, that's my schedule," Raymond joked, then he asked about school and Adragon changed the subject as quickly as possible. His grades were slipping, and he might have asked the old guy for some advice if Elsbeth hadn't been right there at his elbow, never missing a word.

Adragon poured Raymond a glass of white wine and fixed a Perrier with lime for Elsbeth. When she went to the kitchen to check on her Cornish hens, Raymond leaned forward in his chair and lowered his voice.

"I know there must be a young woman in your life," he teased. "Can you tell me who she is, or is it a secret?"

"No one special," Adragon lied, and he felt a stab of anger, wondering if the old man had been spying on him.

"Your room," Raymond explained, "has been dark lately, so I assume you're not watching much TV these nights."

Adragon was pondering what Raymond expected him to say when Elsbeth returned to the room with a tray of hors d'oeuvres. Raymond winked at him behind Elsbeth's back and Adragon added another weird moment to the many others he had experienced during the past few weeks. He made an excuse to leave the room for a few minutes and when he returned his mother and Raymond were sitting close to one another on the pale yellow couch, their heads bent over one of Elsbeth's special blue and

48

white notebooks. She glanced up, her eyes met Adragon's, and he thought she looked rather startled, as if she hadn't really expected him to return to the living room. Later, he realized that she'd looked as if she'd been caught with her hand in the cookie jar. The look wasn't one of surprise; it was guilt.

Still, the reason for her guilt didn't register until days later when Adragon suddenly remembered that Elsbeth never shared the information in her notebooks with anyone, not even her son. They were always kept in her office, hidden away in her desk drawers, and Adragon had often teased her about being paranoid when he caught her locking the desk before they went out to dinner. So what in the hell was she doing sharing her precious notes with Raymond Sadler? Just one more mystery to ponder, Adragon told himself, his last thought before sleeping. In the morning, he had forgotten that there was a mystery.

Chapter Six

As fate would have it, the telephone rang as Adragon was on his way out the door several nights later. He had made a date to take one of the girls he'd met at Friendly's to a movie, and he intended to go through with it, even though the thought of spending an entire evening with the girl didn't inspire much enthusiasm.

The loud foreign noise stopped Adragon in his tracks. The phone had been strangely silent for almost a week, as if some powerful force had paralyzed the dialing fingers of potential callers so that Adragon would not miss the one call for which he waited.

He pulled the kitchen door closed and grabbed the phone on the second ring. Something stuck in his throat, and it was a couple of seconds before he could say "hello."

Del's voice was magical and his name was beautiful.

"Adragon?"

He expelled the air from his lungs with a noisy wheeze. "Yeah, it's me. Hi."

"How are you?"

"Okay, I guess. Yeah, I'm okay."

"I miss you."

He couldn't say that he missed her, too. He couldn't give her that much. Not yet.

"I want to see you," she continued when he said nothing.

"No."

"Please, Adragon. Just see me, let me explain." While she spoke, the memory of her perfect face invaded his mind. Soft strawberry hair falling to her white shoulders. Green eyes, as deep and mysterious as the winter sea. Full, sensuous red lips.

"Okay," he said, interrupting whatever she was saying.

"Okay?"

"Okay, you can see me. But no funny stuff." *Anything you want, you can have anything.*

"I won't do anything you don't want me to do," she promised.

"Tonight?" *Don't beg her. Be cool,* he cautioned himself.

"It's late, and I'm a working girl. Let's make it tomorrow night."

He had never thought about her working, earning a living. To him, she was a siren, a temptress, a being formed of sea mist and moonshine, too beautiful to be real. Now he realized how juvenile his perception of her had been.

"Tomorrow, Adragon?"

"Sure."

"Can you come to my house?"

"Yeah."

"Eight o'clock?"

"Yeah, okay."

"Only what you want, Adragon, I promise."

She hung up, and he spoke into the silence she'd left behind, "I want you, Del. I want you, Del Keelan."

Twenty-four hours. Twenty-four hours and he would see her again, touch her, hold her. Twenty-four hours and she would belong to him. Or maybe he would belong to her. Whatever. He started looking through his wallet for

51

the Friendly girl's phone number. He hated breaking dates at the last minute; his mother had taught him to be a gentleman, and gentlemen didn't go around breaking dates when the girl already had her coat on ready to walk out the door. But he could hardly date a skinny bimbo with a flat chest and a ton of teased hair that would barely fit into his car when he could have Del Keelan, could he?

Del didn't keep her promise not to hurt him, and she didn't do much explaining. None, in fact. Ten minutes after he knocked on her door, Adragon was decidedly unhappy with the way things were going.

"My fingers are sore." He pulled his hand away and resisted when she reached for it again.

"It will only hurt for a minute, then you'll forget about it, I promise."

"You said we'd make love." He came across like a pouty little kid; the sound of his own voice disgusted him, but it was as if he had no control over it. She *had* promised him, hadn't she?

"We will make love, Adragon, and when we do, it will be better than anything you ever imagined."

"I'm not a virgin," he blurted out, a point he had to make before something actually happened. It was true — he had lost his virginity at sixteen, and there had been several repeats of the experience since. But this time it would be different, she was right about that. This time (if there *was* a this time) it would be the stuff that romantic old movies were made of. It would be ecstasy and total surrender and —

"Adragon?"

"What?" He pulled his mind back from his Bogart and Bacall fantasy.

Del pointed one long white finger on her left hand and nicked it with the same sharp instrument she had used to break his skin. He was startled by the suddenness of her move and the violence with which she drew her own blood. A red drop welled to the surface, formed a perfect teardrop shape and fell, disappearing in the crimson folds of her dress. "Drink, Adragon," she whispered, and he edged away from her, shaking his head frantically back and forth.

"Come on, my sweet Adragon, taste my sweet blood," she cajoled, and in that moment he both hated and feared her.

He laughed, a weak, nervous little titter that didn't become him, and tried to reach around her for his jacket, which he had tossed on a spindly white chair.

"Drink, Adragon," she insisted. "It's just a game, remember?"

The words were foolish but the tone of her voice was not to be taken lightly. It mesmerized Adragon, and he felt as if he were sinking, as if he had stumbled into the sea and was on the verge of losing his balance and sliding into deep water. When he did, he knew that he would just keep on falling because there would be no bottom to the depths that flirted with his soul.

"Please." Another perfect drop had formed; she offered it as if it were a treasure. She appeared to be both saddened and angry when he refused.

"I can't," he explained.

"Please," she repeated more emphatically. She squeezed her finger and the red drop rose. Before it had a chance to fall, Del raised her finger to Adragon's lips, and smeared them with the sticky red liquid. His resistance fell away. He could no longer remember his reason for refusing her. He took the drop of blood on the tip of his tongue and drew it into his mouth. He felt a shock of pleasure, as if he had committed a sexual act, as if he had touched her most private, secret place with his mouth. He knew that a blush had spread to his face but at the moment that was the least of his worries. He was much more concerned with his body's reaction to Del's generosity.

Her blood was sweet, sweeter than candy, and he let that sweetness fill his mind and blot out the horror of what he was doing. She withdrew her finger from his mouth, and his eyes followed it hungrily until she relented. She suckled him, and gave him nourishment of a kind he hadn't known he needed until he tasted her blood. They rested then, but he knew it wasn't over, and he was right.

The second time it was easier; Del made it easier. She coaxed him down on the big white couch and knelt before him. His mind filled and overflowed with fantasies of wild, unspeakable sexual acts, acts that she could perform from her position on her knees just inches from that most perverted part of his anatomy. The fantasy heightened when her silky red blouse slid off her smooth white shoulder; Adragon tried to raise his hand to touch her but his arms were heavy, weighted.

She caressed him lightly, ran cool, experienced fingers up his arms, across his bare chest (for less than a second, he wondered what had happened to his shirt — it didn't matter). She bent her head, red hair brushing his face, and bit at his nipples with bared teeth, moved her red lips to the tender flesh of his neck and left her mark there.

"You're so smooth," she purred, "skin like a baby's behind." Maybe it was meant to be a compliment, but he didn't take it that way. He wanted to be offended, wanted to mourn the fact that he was years away from thick masculine body hair and scratchy stubble (*light* years, since he seemed to have inherited all of his genes from his mother, rather than his absent father). But his lips wouldn't move to form the words, to tell her that she had hurt his pride, and soon he forgot to remember.

When Del was finished with him, when she had drawn a minute amount of blood from his fingers for the second time that night, working them one by one, sucking them hard enough to bring him to orgasm, she traded places with him. She still didn't offer him her body, just her fingers, but it was a hell of a lot better than nothing at all.

Adragon took the middle finger of her right hand and raised it to his lips. It was beautiful: skin so white, blood so red pulsing just beneath the fine parchment, moving through the delicate tracery of veins. The tip of her finger was sensuous, round, flushed to a warm pink. He held onto her hand and raised his eyes to look into hers, which were a shade of green he would have thought impossible to mix on a palette, even if he had every hue in the world to work with. She stared back at him, encouraging him.

Del wanted to pierce her finger for him, but he had to do it himself. Not with the instrument she offered; with his teeth. He did it gently and wantonly. He took the fat drop of her blood onto the tip of his tongue and licked it slowly into his mouth, closed his lips around it. He savored that single drop as he had never savored exotic food or expensive champagne.

Again, her blood didn't taste anything like he would have imagined blood would taste, and nothing like the blood (pretend blood?) that he had taken from the tiny gold spoon. Del's blood was sweet, warm and sweet and addictive. He knew that already. When she offered her finger again, he opened his mouth wide and sucked on it eagerly, a baby thirsting for his mother's milk. He drew harder and he knew that he was hurting her, but he couldn't stop, and he didn't until she spoke his name several times and finally, forcibly pushed him away.

"I'm sorry, Del." It was a half-truth, and she probably knew it, but he ran with it. "I don't know what happened, I've never—"

Adragon stopped speaking abruptly and stared at Del in disbelief. She was laughing, her head thrown back, her beautiful hair swirling across her shoulders, her red lips parted.

55

"You're wonderful," she told him when she could catch her breath again.

She might have expected Adragon to laugh along with her, but his reaction was fast and furious. "You're making fun of me," he accused, forcing her to hurriedly rearrange her face.

"You are," she said in a completely different tone of voice, "you're wonderful," and she began to undress him slowly and to even more slowly make love to him with her hands, until he was trembling and barely coherent.

"I love you, Del," he murmured, as he came for the third time in as many hours. But if she heard him, she pretended that she didn't.

When he arrived home at 2:00 A.M., the door to Elsbeth's quarters was closed, and no light seeped out from behind it. Adragon went to bed happy, sure that the late hour of his return went unnoticed. It wasn't until morning that he found out that Elsbeth had been awake, waiting for the sound of his key in the lock.

"Where were you last night?" she asked, letting her reading glasses slide down on her nose so that she could peer at him over the top of the frame.

"Out with the guys," he lied.

"Out where?"

"Just out—does it matter?"

"Don't answer my questions with questions, Adragon. You're only seventeen, and I'm still your mother. As long as you're living in my house—"

"*Your* house?"

"That's right, *my* house."

"Do you want me to leave?"

"You *can't* leave. I will remind you again that you're only seventeen years old, a minor in the eyes of the law."

"Who gives a shit? If you don't want me here, I'm sure you can find a way around the law."

"Just drop it, Adragon, I don't want to hear your hurt

little boy act." She leaned across the table to look up at him, and he had no doubt that she was deadly serious. "Wherever you've been spending your time, mark it off your agenda. I want you here, in this house, before midnight every night, unless I give you specific permission to stay out later. Do you understand?"

He refused to give her the satisfaction of acknowledging her ridiculous order. He was, after all, seventeen, not a child to be bossed around and given deadlines. He stomped out of the kitchen, slammed the door and ran down the steps to the beach, his mother's strident voice following him with more demands, more warnings.

Adragon was so angry that he felt like yelling and striking out at something, or someone. But the only person in sight was Raymond, jogging slowly across the sand, looking thin and trim in powder blue sweats.

"Adragon, my boy —" The older man raised his hand in greeting, and veered off course to move closer to his young neighbor.

"Hi, Ray."

"Come along and keep me company while I indulge my aging cardiovascular system."

"Sure."

Raymond slowed his pace and turned to glance at Adragon. "Problems?" he asked.

"Just Mom. She's not in a very good mood this morning."

"Don't tell me she found you out." Raymond turned his head away before he smiled, but Adragon caught him.

"What do you mean?" he asked, but he already knew: Raymond was onto him.

"I haven't been sleeping too well lately. I'm afraid I heard you come home last night."

Adragon shrugged and tried not to look like the cat that ate the canary.

"New girl, huh?"

57

"Yeah, sort of."

"An older woman I'll bet. Good for you, my boy." Raymond turned his head and winked at Adragon, without slowing his pace. "I've got an idea. Suppose I drop by and see Elsbeth this evening. Maybe I can put in a good word for you."

"Well, sure," Adragon answered doubtfully, "anything you can do to help."

Raymond slapped him on the back and picked up speed, leaving Adragon to fall behind. The man turned back toward his house, and soon he was out of sight, although Adragon was running through the wet sand as fast as his legs would carry him.

The kitchen was empty when he got home, and he could hear the click-click of Elsbeth's fingers on the computer keyboard when he listened at her door. He tiptoed around the house for most of the day, dreading another face-to-face with his mother but when he finally saw her again, at the dinner table, she was pleasant and forgiving.

It took him a few minutes to figure it out: the argument had scared his mother, probably as much as it had scared him. What would she do if he walked out on her? She would be devastated. And that's exactly what he'd do if she pushed him too far. Wouldn't he? Yes, he would. For Del Keelan, yes, he would walk out on his mother without a moment's hesitation.

Chapter Seven

There was something not-quite-right about Adragon's budding relationship with Del, but he chose not to think about it. In fact, he pushed it to the back of his mind and buried it there so that he wouldn't have to examine it too closely. The blood thing, the finger thing, that was what bothered him. He was only seventeen, after all, and he pretended to be sophisticated, to have been around. But the truth was that he wasn't entirely sure things like that weren't a part of normal adult relationships.

In high school, there had been a lot of locker room gossip about "older women" and their perverted sexual habits. Fingers, tongues, teeth, and even kitchen implements were mentioned in connection with their forbidden practices, most of which Adragon had never quite understood.

Don't kid yourself, Adragon, a part of him warned, *this vampire thing isn't normal, and you know it.*

It nagged at him until he finally had to admit that it worried him a lot, Del and Elsbeth and all the other people pretending they were vampires. Pretending so hard they really believed it? Who knew.

For Del Keelan, to sleep with Del Keelan, if he had to pretend to be a vampire and do the vampire thing, he'd do it. No problem.

59

There was one other thing that bothered him: he kept remembering the taste of her blood on his tongue, the sweetness, the way it made him feel, grown-up and powerful, like he could do anything. Yeah, that was really weird, but that, too, he shoved into a dark recess of his mind and hid it from the light of day.

After his run-in with Elsbeth, fear of another encounter kept Adragon away from Del for one day and one night. But by the end of the second day, he was crazy with desire for her. He knocked on her door feeling so juvenile, his palms sweaty, his deodorant working overtime, his heart tripping in his chest.

In spite of his doing everything he could to please her, it was to be another night of frustration and unfulfilled desire. Adragon's exploration of Del's voluptuous body was limited to cupping her breasts and stroking her thighs. Under his breath, he used every dirty word he had learned growing up in Asbury Park, in the company of the tough Jersey Shore lower class, to describe what he wanted to do to her. Aloud, he dared say only two words, *"Please, Del."*

"In time, sweet Adragon," she promised, and he carried the promise with him when he left her at midnight, sated with her blood. In his own bed, in what he now thought of as Elsbeth's house, he found his own release.

Thoughts of Del Keelan filled his every waking moment. It seemed only natural that he dream of her at night and savor again the taste of her blood as they played the vampire games she had taught him.

As for Elsbeth, Adragon and his mother lived in her house together, yet separate, and mention was never made of the Society of Vampires, or of that part of her life she chose not to share with him.

On a Saturday night in mid-December, Adragon came out of his room at dinnertime to find the dining room empty, the kitchen table set for one.

"You're not feeding me tonight?" he joked, aware of a

strange rumbling in the pit of his stomach that had nothing to do with hunger.

"I'm dining out," Elsbeth answered, turning from her position by the door, where she had been gazing out at the deserted beach. She twirled, and Adragon's heart did a funny little flip-flop. She was wearing a silky black dress that covered her from her neck to below her knees while managing to reveal far too much of her slim, youthful figure.

"You have a date?" he asked, feeling resentful.

"Is that so totally unbelievable?"

"You look great." He opened the fridge and spotted his dinner: a turkey club sandwich on wheat, hold the mayo. Good old Mom, even hot for a date, she didn't once forget her little boy's diet.

"Who's the lucky guy?" he asked casually. He lifted a jar of Weight Watcher's mayonnaise from the shelf and Elsbeth hurried forward with a teaspoon to measure it out.

"Our next door neighbor," she answered, and turned her back to return the jar to the refrigerator. "Iced tea?" She turned back to face him, and Adragon had to ask her to repeat the question.

"Iced tea, yeah, great. Ray?"

"Ray, yes. Don't look at me that way, Adragon, we're only going out to dinner."

"You never dress that way when I take you out to dinner."

She stared at him just long enough to make him feel uncomfortable. He knew that his face was red, and he coughed to cover the reason for his embarrassment.

"Sorry," he mumbled, "I have no business grilling you about your dates. I forgot my place." He brushed past her, grabbed his car keys off the counter where he'd thrown them, and slammed out the door. "Have fun," he called back to his mother but he didn't mean it. He fervently hoped that she'd have a miserable evening.

Adragon ordered a burger and fries at Wendy's, purposely breaking his diet and shooting his sugar level sky-high. "That'll teach her," he told his reflection in the rear-view mirror when he returned to the car, and he laughed for the first time that evening.

In a better mood, he drove to Del's condo and pounded on the door for ten minutes before he admitted to himself that she wasn't home. He was halfway back to Elsbeth's house when the thought struck him: The Society of Vampires was holding a meeting tonight. Del and Elsbeth both out on a Saturday night, neither of them interested in spending the evening with him, both of them sneaking around trying to avoid telling him where they were going. Lies! They had told him lies to escape from him so that they could meet behind his back and do the vampire thing. When he'd called Del earlier, she'd said that she was feeling ill, that she'd call him if she felt well enough to have him come over.

"Fuck you, Elsbeth," he shouted out the window of his little car. "Fuck you, Delphine."

He ran up and down the beach until his legs shook and his blood pounded in his temples, then he went home to sleep, with his last waking breath of the day damning to hell both of the women he loved.

The next morning, Elsbeth was already in her office when Adragon came in from his run on the beach. He was glad he didn't have to face her before he'd taken his insulin shot and poured his coffee. In the light of day, he felt foolish for the way he'd acted the night before, but that didn't mean he was ready to forgive her. He still felt like grilling her about her "date" and gathering information to use against her.

He took two sips of his coffee before he walked back through the house and rapped on her door. He pushed it open without waiting for her to invite him in, the first time he'd ever done that. She raised her eyes from the computer screen and seemed to have trouble focusing on his face. For just a moment, her alarm at the intrusion was reflected in her eyes.

"Where did you go last night?" he demanded. Without waiting for an answer, he grabbed her arms and pulled her roughly out of the chair, scattering manuscript pages, finally getting her full attention.

"Answer me," he yelled, "where the hell were you?"

"Let go of me and stop shouting. Who the hell do you think you are?" She jerked away from him, cold and angry, as eerily calm as the sea behind the drawn drapes. She gave him a hard shove toward the door, and he momentarily lost his balance, which made him want to throttle her. He grabbed her by her short curly hair and twisted her head back. He wanted her to punch him, wanted her to fight. But instead of lashing out at him, she met his eyes with hers, still that awful calm. "I'm warning you," she said quietly, and Adragon dropped his hands to his sides.

"Okay, okay." He threw his hands up in the air in a conciliatory gesture. "You're my mother. I worry about you."

"Nice try, Adragon, but you can't fool me that way. I know you too well."

"I don't know what you're talking about, Mother."

"You know where I was last night. You know because you followed me, didn't you?"

"I didn't follow you, Elsbeth, I just figured it out."

She smiled then but it wasn't a motherly smile. "There was a meeting of the Society, Adragon. I didn't tell you because I thought you might resent my going without you, and I guess I was right."

"How am I supposed to react to your little meetings, Mother, would you like to tell me that? You doll yourself up to look like a whore and go off to suck blood with a bunch of sick losers and I'm supposed to just sit here and read a book until you get back? Is that what I'm supposed to do? Is that what your vampire rule book says I'm supposed to do?"

Elsbeth raised her dark eyebrows and the gesture irritated Adragon so badly that he almost succumbed to the desire to strike her.

"Sick losers?" she asked, her eyes cold, her mouth smiling. "Is that what you call them? Does that include your little vampire friend, Del Keelan?"

"Cut the crap, Elsbeth," he told her, again barely overcoming the urge to knock her across the room, "that vampire shit's getting on my nerves."

"Maybe it's not crap," she said the word as though she could taste it.

"You know something? You're as crazy as they are. Crazier. Maybe I should hire a lawyer and have you committed."

He backed out of the door and stalked down the hallway to his own quarters. He was almost there when he heard Elsbeth close her door and slide the lock into place. After that, all he heard was her laughter.

He went to see Del that night with every intention of asking her about the Society's most recent meeting, but the minute she opened the door, he forgot everything except his desire for her. Her robe was silky, the same luminescent shade of green as her eyes. Her face was free of makeup, her hair damp from the shower, and the robe clung to her body, as if she had thrown it on without bothering to towel herself dry.

She was so beautiful that Adragon could hardly stand to look at her; it was like staring at the noonday sun. Inside the stark white living room, she circled him, backing him across the room toward the couch. He dodged her and moved over to the windows, stared out at the gray winter sea.

"Adragon?"

"Yeah?"

"Turn around."

He wanted to say *No;* he wanted to bolt, run out of the

apartment, out of the building, out of her life. He wanted her more than he wanted his next breath. He was afraid of her.

"There are no such things as vampires, are there?" He turned, almost against his will, and asked again when she didn't answer immediately. "Are there?"

She was standing in a shaft of light that fell from a tall lamp in the far corner of the room. Her robe lay in a green puddle at her feet.

It was hard, but he lowered his eyes until all he could see was the carpet, a great, white sea beneath his feet. "Answer my question, Del."

"Are you afraid of vampires, Adragon?" she asked in a faraway voice. "Are you afraid of me?"

"I just don't know why you want to pretend to be a vampire."

"I don't pretend, Adragon. That's what I am."

He shook his head and made a sweeping gesture with his hands, more definitely negative than a simple "no."

"You don't have to believe me. I don't care about that . . ."

"Oh, Del . . ."

". . . but if you don't believe me, I don't understand why it worries you so much, my pretending. Haven't you ever played make-believe? Haven't you ever wanted to be someone else, someone more exciting than your everyday self?"

"Let me make love to you, Del." He let his eyes drink in the exquisite perfection of her body, and he knew that this was a once in a lifetime night. Nothing as beautiful as Del Keelan would ever happen to him again.

She started to shake her head, and a white flash of anger gave Adragon courage. "I'm not going to beg anymore, Del. If the answer is no, then I think I'd better stop wasting my time."

Her eyes followed him as he crossed the room, as he put his hand on the doorknob. He was turning it when she spoke, saving him. "I want you to move in with me, Adragon. I want you to live with me."

He had trouble hearing the end of the sentence and the words that followed. Something screamed in his ears, some until now only imagined harbinger of joy or fear, or something else, something he couldn't identify and didn't want to remember.

". . . leave her tonight," Del was saying, "go home and tell her that you're leaving. She won't try to stop you. Come back to me and I'll make you happy, in a way that no other woman can. I'll give you everything you need, Adragon, everything."

He shook his head and backed away from her outstretched arms, as if he had just discovered that she had two heads. "No . . . no."

"I want to show you how to live, Adragon. I want to show you how to be a man."

He was still shaking his head, and now he raised his arms to keep distance between them. "I'm not twenty-one, Del. She won't let me get away with it."

"She won't want to make trouble, trust me."

His laughter was totally without warmth or humor. "You don't know Elsbeth very well."

"I know her better than you think."

"Did you talk to her at the meeting last night? Did you two have a cozy little talk over cocktails? Blood cocktails?" The anger he had pushed away returned full force, and he forgot his resolve to let it go.

"Is that what you're angry about? The meeting? Are you angry because I left you on your own for one night? That's very childish, Adragon. Our relationship will never work unless you act with a little more maturity."

"Our relationship?" he asked with more sarcasm than he intended. "Do we have a 'relationship,' Del?"

There was real sadness in her eyes when she answered, and he wished that he could go back and start the evening over. "I thought we were working on a relationship, Adragon. But maybe I was reading something into it that wasn't really there."

"No, no, you weren't. I'm sorry, Del, I didn't mean to hurt you. You mean so much to me." He floundered, and the expression in the woman's eyes changed.

"Then prove it," she challenged.

"Oh, God." He surrendered without a struggle and pulled her into his arms, where she fit so perfectly. Her skin was smooth and cool to the touch, and he buried his face in her shoulder. She smelled of soap and baby powder, everything pure and good, except — He remembered the nights she had made him suck her blood, and something sour crept up his throat and into his mouth. Blood . . . soap and baby powder and blood, that's what she smelled like.

Adragon was suddenly painfully aroused. He pressed his body against Del's, begging her with body language.

"Tell her, Adragon," she whispered, moving against him, "tell her you're moving out. Do it for me. For us."

"Don't torture me like this. I need you, Del."

"Not as much as I need you, Adragon." She took his hand and ran her index finger over the tip of his middle finger, then followed the path of her finger with her tongue.

"Oh no," he moaned, "not the vampire thing again. Come on, Del, I need to make love the human way tonight."

He expected her to become angry, but she didn't. She smiled and urged him toward the door, applying a new degree of torturous pressure against his body with every step they took. In the hall, she kissed his cheek and left him waiting for the elevator, his head swimming with confusion, his penis throbbing with desire.

Chapter Eight

Adragon sat in the car for a long time before he even raised his eyes and looked up at the windows of the house. Elsbeth was home, her car was there, almost invisible in the shadows of the pilings. He glanced at his watch and then back to the windows. It was late; she was probably sleeping. With any luck, he could pack a small bag, sneak out, drive back to Del's condo, and wait for the shit to hit the fan in the morning when Elsbeth discovered that he was gone.

He took a deep breath before he stepped out of the car, closed the driver's side door as gently as possible, and tip-toed up the steps to the kitchen door. The key grated as it turned in the lock, and Adragon flinched, waiting for his mother's "Who's there? Is that you, Adragon?" It never came, and he slipped soundlessly into the house and down the hallway.

He took a small overnight bag from the top shelf in the hall closet, being careful not to creak the folding doors. He opened the bag on his bed and tossed in underwear, socks, and jeans. On his way to the closet for his shirts, he literally ran into his mother. She stood in the middle of the room, arms crossed on her chest, eyes dark with anger.

"Where do you think you're going?" she asked, and

Adragon would have given anything to turn back the clock, to be able to say "Nowhere, Mom, it's a joke. Get it?" He could have done that once, but he couldn't go back to that now. He could never go back to that time again. He was betraying his mother, and there was a finality in that, an awful finality.

"I'm moving out." That was the only answer he could give her.

"Empty that suitcase and go to bed. We'll talk about this in the morning."

She was closing his door behind her when he cleared his throat and spoke again. "No, we won't, damn it. We'll talk about it now."

"Adragon, what's your problem? Didn't you hear what I said?"

"I heard you."

"Then put the damned suitcase away and stop trying to irritate me before you succeed."

Elsbeth put her hands on her hips and took a phony military stance that annoyed Adragon to no end.

"Don't try to throw your weight around, Mother, this isn't West Point. I'm moving out, and there's nothing you can do to stop me."

"Don't bet on it, little boy. You're only seventeen years old. There are laws."

"So call the police." He took a wide berth around Elsbeth on his way to the closet, grabbed the first things he saw, two long-sleeved shirts and two sweaters that didn't match them. Back at the bed, he crammed them all into the little bag and had it zipped before he remembered that he had forgotten toilet articles, and decided that he didn't care. All he cared about was his escape. Maybe she actually would call the police on him. He lifted the bag and walked toward her.

"You take one step out of this house and I will call the police, you little bastard."

"If I'm a bastard, what does that make you?"

"How dare you talk to me like that," she screamed, and dove at him, pulling at his leather jacket, trying to rip it. "How dare you threaten to leave my house, after all I've done for you. Just where do you plan to go? Tell me, you bastard, where in the hell can you go? You don't have any money, you don't have anything without me."

She ran out of steam and he pushed her hands away, stood there and faced her with what he knew was a nasty, shit-eating smile. "I'm moving in with Del Keelan, Mother. Aren't you proud of me for finding someone to take me in?"

He hadn't been going to tell her, and he wouldn't have if she hadn't called him a bastard. The minute he mentioned Del's name, he knew it was a mistake.

Elsbeth's eyes widened, her mouth gaped open, and Adragon wished himself away from there, but his wish didn't come true. He was forced to stand there just inches away from her while she laughed uproariously, then stopped suddenly and grabbed the overnight case from Adragon's hands. Before he could react, she had dumped the contents on his bed.

"You're not going anyplace," she screamed shrilly, "least of all to that whore's house."

"I told you," Adragon answered with a calm that surprised him, "I'm moving in with Del."

"Do you know what that woman is? Do you have any idea what she wants from you?"

Was there real fear in his mother's eyes now, or was Adragon simply seeing what he wanted to see there? Whatever message Elsbeth's eyes contained, her son ignored it.

"All Del has to do is ask for anything she wants from me," he answered boldly.

Elsbeth's hand shot out so quickly that he took the slap's full power, and his body rocked from the impact. He didn't think; he reacted. His hand connected with his mother's cheek with a sharp crack, and she started to scream uncontrollably. One second too late, he was profoundly sorry for his action, totally ashamed of himself. Adragon had had numerous verbal sparring matches with Elsbeth since he reached adolescence, but he had never raised his hand to her before, and he could count on the fingers of one hand the times his mother had slapped him during the course of his entire life.

Her face was red, the outline of his palm a perfect white print on the delicate flesh. He thought he would die of mortification. He couldn't believe that he had actually struck his mother, his beloved Elsbeth.

"Oh shit, Elsbeth, I'm sorry, I didn't mean to hit you."

"You may leave now, Adragon," she whispered without meeting his eyes. "Please lock the door behind you."

She turned and strode regally from the room, magnificent in her self-possession. He was impressed by her self-control, more so because she usually had so little control when she was angry. He wanted to apologize again, to hold her in his arms, to kiss the soft curve of her cheek which bore the ugly proof of his own lack of control.

His door closed softly and he was alone. Terribly alone. Del Keelan was a fantasy, a dream that might never come true for him, and for her he had alienated his mother.

Adragon had no choice but to repack his bag and leave the house he had helped Elsbeth design for their shared pleasure and convenience. He had once thought that he would live there always, and never leave the woman he had loved totally since his infancy. Tears filled his eyes and threatened to run down his cheeks but he held them back with the thought that Del waited for him in the green silk robe that clung to her body like a second skin. Del and her promise to make love to him drove him down the steps to his car.

That night the fantasy was fulfilled. He was only seventeen years old, but he realized that he had come to a plateau in his life. He wondered how the rest of his life could ever measure up to the magic of those few hours. When she opened the door, she was still wearing the robe, but her hair had dried and hung in reddish-gold waves over her shoulders, cloud-soft and intoxicatingly fragrant. He sat his suitcase down just inside the door and reached for her.

"It's done."

She took his hands and placed them on her breasts under the robe. To his surprise, her body was icy cold, so cold that he imagined the blood that pounded in her chest would not be warm, human blood. For just a moment, he was afraid, and he would have backed away from her, but it was impossible.

She kissed him then and with her cold lips still touching his, whispered, "Warm me, Adragon." She moved her lips to his neck and he jerked away.

"Are you still afraid of me?"

"Hell no. What kind of a man do you think I am?"

"You're just a boy, but I'll teach you how to be a man tonight."

"Maybe I can teach you something in return."

"Maybe you can."

Del let him take the initiative in their lovemaking. He stripped the robe from her body and lifted her in his arms. He carried her to the bedroom, and this time she held back nothing, but Adragon was not fooled. He knew that she was still in control.

Hours later, the reality of what he had done struck him hard.

"I shouldn't have slapped her. She's probably called the police by now."

"Stop worrying. She won't call the police. She'll want to keep a low profile."

"Oh, God, Elsbeth will never forgive me. Never."

"Do you realize that you're literally wringing your hands?"

"Don't laugh at me, Del, this isn't funny."

"Lighten up, Adragon, your mother's been using you for years. It's about time you declared your independence. Maybe she'll find herself a boyfriend if you stay away long enough. Maybe she'll even start to grow up."

"What do you have against my mother?" Adragon propped himself up on his elbow so that he could watch her face while she answered. He always had the feeling that she knew Elsbeth better than she pretended to know her.

Instead of answering, she stood and stretched, then leaned over to kiss him.

"You are incredible, but I can't —"

"Of course, you can." The sound of her laughter reminded him of the tiny silver bells Elsbeth had hung in the windows of their house. *Her* house. He pulled Del down on top of him and buried his face in her hair.

The next time Adragon woke up, he was alone in the bed. The sheets were damp and twisted, the red satin coverlet balled on the white carpet. He found his watch on the nightstand; the hands showed a few minutes before noon. He moaned, rolled out of bed, and dug his Jockey shorts out of the smelly bedclothes. As soon as he stood up, he had to admit that he wasn't feeling too well. He was on his way to the kitchen to take his shot when he realized that he hadn't brought his insulin with him. Panic set in, and he had to sit down at the kitchen counter and make up a game plan.

Call Elsbeth, or call his doctor, or maybe the pharmacy had a refill of his prescription on file. You didn't need a prescription to buy insulin, but you *did* need one to buy needles. No, better idea: call Raymond. The guy was a doctor; he'd know what to do. Maybe he'd just walk over to Elsbeth's house and pick up the small kit he kept packed for emergencies: spare bottle of Novolin 70/30 insulin, extra Tes-Tape, alcohol wipes, and several packets of micro-fine needles.

Adragon sat at the bar in his undershorts and dialed Ray Sadler's number, let it ring until the man picked up. It was only after Ray had promised to come up with the quickest solution to the problem and call Adragon back, that he noticed the table-setting and the sheet of white notepaper.

"Good morning, sweet Adragon," it read. "Think of me while you eat your breakfast . . . coffee in the canister, bread in the bread box, milk in the 'fridge. I'll call. Del."

The phone rang while he was pouring Total Corn Flakes into a blue bowl, but it wasn't Del, it was Raymond.

"I've spoken to your mother, Adragon, and I'm afraid you've misjudged her badly. She's bringing your medication over to me now — I can see her from the window. She wants me to deliver it to you immediately. She's very concerned for your health."

"She wasn't concerned for my health last night."

"Don't be a child, Adragon. That type of behavior doesn't become you."

"I'm sorry, Ray."

"I'm on my way with the medicine, my boy. I should be there in thirty minutes or so. Elsbeth's at the door now."

"Ray, wait! Do you know where I am?"

"I know exactly where you are, Adragon."

When he opened the door in answer to Raymond's knock a half hour later, Adragon asked the question, "How did you know where I was?"

"Your mother told me, of course."

"She doesn't know where Del lives."

Raymond scrutinized the younger man's face before answering. "I think you're exaggerating the importance of a very easily accessible bit of information, Adragon,

74

but if you must know, I had some business dealings with Miss Keelan a few years back."

"What kind of business was that, Ray?"

"You're becoming very tiresome, my boy. I'm beginning to feel as if this is an interrogation. Very well, I sold her this condo. I bought it when it was first built, with the idea that I might eventually sell my house and move in here. When I decided to keep the house, I advertised for a buyer, and Miss Keelan contacted me. Does that satisfy you, or do you have further questions?"

"I'm sorry, Ray." Adragon rubbed at his forehead and stepped away from the door so that the other man could enter the room.

"Headache? Well, I have your insulin here, and I'll write you a new prescription for your needles, then you'd best telephone your own physician for an appointment. I'm sure there's no need to tell you that Elsbeth is worried sick about the possibility that you might neglect your health."

"I'm sure," Adragon mumbled under his breath, as he led Raymond down the hallway to the kitchen, where he watched as Adragon prepared the injection and plunged the needle into the flesh of his upper arm.

"Okay," Adragon breathed, "I know it's all in my mind, but I feel better already." Raymond nodded, wrote out a prescription for needles, since Adragon's supply was low, and prepared to leave. At the door, he turned and once more carefully examined the boy's face. "It's none of my business, Adragon, but this trouble with your mother—" The look on the other's face stopped him. He shook his head sadly, squeezed the boy's shoulder, and stepped into the elevator, leaving Adragon alone again. It seemed to him that whatever woman he chose to live with, he ended up spending one hell of a lot of time alone.

The hours he actually spent with Del passed far too quickly. It was as if she was able to distort time, and make an entire evening disappear in minutes. She was almost too much for his seventeen-year-old constitution: stunning, exotic, strange. Her entire apartment was decorated in stark white, with splashes of crimson. Adragon thought that the white was supposed to be her milky skin, and the red her blood: her bloodred lips and nails, the red clothing that she favored, blood dripping on pale, colorless flesh.

Del usually came to him dressed in red or white, or a combination of both. She wound her thin white arms around his body and kissed him with bloodless lips that grew full and red as their weird lovemaking progressed. Adragon often shuddered when he kissed her back for the first time any particular evening, dreading what was to come, then welcoming it. She pricked his fingers, then moved on to puncture his wrists. He watched his lifeblood flow into her mouth, and he grew weak as she grew stronger. Afterward, he felt needed and used, vitally important and totally disposable. Then it was his turn, and all the reverse feelings came into play. He was using her then, and he knew it, even though he adamantly refused to admit his dependency.

She glowed afterward, for nearly twenty-four hours, with bright, shining eyes and glossy lips that required no cosmetic products to heighten their luster. He knew that he was giving Del life, and it was the most important thing he did from day to day, from night to night. Still, he refused to acknowledge the name of the thing she was, and he ignored the nagging fear that she was changing him into a creature like herself. Further, he wouldn't let himself think about what she had done for sustenance before he came along.

In the days that followed his move into her apartment, Adragon fell into a routine of sorts. He slept late, took his insulin injection and ate breakfast alone, went for long, slow walks on the beach or stared at a silent TV screen until Del appeared at the door. She usually brought their dinner in take-out cartons: Chinese, Italian, fish, burgers, nothing more imaginative.

It didn't matter what they ate. Del consumed very little food, and Adragon seemed to have lost his appetite. He didn't know whether he should be taking the same dosage of insulin, but he assumed that the fact that he was eating less and exercising less balanced each other out. When he mentioned it to Del and asked for her advice, she only smiled and told him to "lighten up, Adragon, it isn't that important anymore." Whatever that meant.

The fact didn't escape him that as he continued to drink minute amounts of Del's blood, the less he craved normal human sustenance.

Vampire! The word exploded in his mind and he fought it off with a vengeance. More than once the added factor of Elsbeth's part in the deterioration of his humanity invaded his thoughts. If only she had never accepted the Society's invitation . . . if only she had not taken him with her. But if he had never met Del, would he ever have fallen in love with such a beautiful creature? Since he knew now that he was in love with her, he dared to ask her questions.

"Why was she allowed to take me with her to that first meeting? That's just not their style, is it? I mean, they're so into secrecy."

"She insisted. She said she wouldn't go if you couldn't escort her."

"And your leader, whoever he is, accepted that?"

"You have no idea how badly they — *we* wanted her. She's going to write a book about us, a book that will show us as we really are."

"She's writing it now." Adragon thought of the long hours Elsbeth spent behind her closed door, the look of absolute concentration on her lovely face when she emerged from her cocoon.

"Yes, she is," Del answered, "and when it's published, people will begin to understand us."

"Can she really do that?" He was in awe; she was, after all, his mother.

"Oh, yes, she can do that."

"Why can't I join?" It was the question he had sworn to himself he wouldn't ask.

"Sweet Adragon, you're not ready yet."

"And Elsbeth is?" He pushed Del's hands away, even though he knew that refusal would cost him more than it would cost her.

"In ways, yes. Let it go, Adragon, your time will come, I promise you."

They didn't make love that night, and there was no exchange of blood. The next night, Del fell asleep while Adragon was in the shower, and he shook her roughly awake, then accused her of having another lover.

"You need blood, I know you do," he screamed at her. "If you're not getting it from me, then you're getting it from someone else."

"If you'll stop yelling, I'll explain a little bit about my nature," she answered coldly, and Adragon listened.

"I can have human babies, Adragon. I have all the necessary female parts. I also have a menstrual cycle. But it's different for vampires, longer and more intense. For a week every month it's absolutely necessary for me to get more rest, to keep from tiring myself."

"And to get your blood," he added.

"Yes, that, too."

Adragon stared into her eyes until she told him what he wanted to know. "There is no one else, no one but you. I have a supply in the back of the freezer for these special times."

"Better than mine?" Was that really his voice asking that question, acting as if he were jealous because she found other blood more tasty than his?

"Not better, not as good, not as sweet."

"Then why?"

"You have diabetes, Adragon. For just a few days every month I need untainted blood."

"You think my blood is tainted?" He growled and grabbed her by her upper arms, threatened to pull her out of the bed and onto the floor.

"Oh, God, bad choice of words. Not tainted, no, never, just not the type of blood I need right now. Please try to understand. If it was my choice, if it was something I could control . . . but it isn't."

He slammed her body back onto the bed and started to dress quickly: jeans, T-shirt, leather jacket, feet jammed into sneakers without socks. He heard her crying as he raced out of the apartment, but he couldn't stop. He couldn't help himself. He knew what he needed, and he hoped his instincts would show him where to find it.

Chapter Nine

Without thinking about where he would go, Adragon drove to Asbury Park, the scene of so much frustration and confusion in his childhood. It was there he had hated his mother for a few short minutes each time he had to leave the beach and travel back to their tiny, stifling apartment. Then only minutes later, indulging in the rare treat of a hot dog or an ice cream cone, he would love her so much that he thought his love would break his heart. He had loved her in return for her love, which shone in her sad eyes when she promised him that it wouldn't always be that way, that someday they would have everything they needed and more.

Her promise had come true: she had written a book and sold it, then sold a second and a third, and everything in their lives had been altered. The only thing that had changed for the worst was the amount of time his mother spent with him, and he had prided himself on understanding that her career was her first priority. They built the house on the shore, and Elsbeth spent more and more time in her bedroom, the clickity-clack of her old typewriter lulling her teenage son to sleep almost every night of the week. But Adragon suddenly had every material thing he had ever coveted or desired, and that helped ease the pain of all the long hours he spent alone. He was, after all, a very material boy.

It was drizzling in Asbury Park this cold night in December, and Adragon pushed the memories of his lonely years to the back of his mind and concentrated on the present.

He parked the Mustang on a side street and stepped out onto the rain-slick sidewalk. He turned up the collar of his leather jacket. It didn't offer him much protection from the rain, but it did shadow his face and give him a little privacy from the streetwise punks who tried to look into his eyes and figure their chances.

Every time he came to Asbury Park, he shuddered to think that he might run into someone he knew from his childhood; still, the town attracted him like a magnet. He couldn't stay away. Elsbeth had gotten him out of the small apartment as soon as her third book sold, when he was only thirteen, but it would just be his luck to run into someone who remembered him, someone who might recognize him and be able to identify him if — If what? If he dragged someone into a dark alley and drank their blood? No!

Yes. Because, oh God, that's what he wanted to do.

Keeping his head bowed, he shuffled from block to block, into the rougher neighborhoods, away from the light. There were women on the streets — women standing in the drizzling rain in tight, short skirts, women tottering up and down curbs in three-inch heels. They looked bedraggled and ridiculous to Adragon, and they certainly weren't his type, but he envisioned their white throats beneath the turned-up collars of their cheap coats, and he wanted them. Whenever he passed within a few feet of one of them, he heard her blood beating in her throat. He saw her chest rising and falling in rhythm with her pulse, and his desire grew with every hammering beat of a prostitute's heart.

He wanted them, all of them, although he knew that

81

they were soiled with dried semen, and he was aware of the potential for disease they carried between their legs and on their lips. He wanted them, although he knew that they had come back to the streets from their short-time rooms, maybe not for the first time tonight. He was forced to clench his fists and jam his hands into the pockets of his jacket to prevent himself from grabbing one of the unclean girls as she passed close to him.

On the darkest street, he lost control for nearly fatal seconds. A growl rose from deep in his throat. He bared his teeth and sprang across the narrow sidewalk at a skinny child-woman. She screamed, but there was no one to hear, and Adragon felt as if he were god, as if this pitiful life was his to spare or take, as he saw fit.

The girl's hands were cold, but her neck was warm under the scarf he ripped away. She fought him tooth and nail, but she was no match for him; he easily threw her to the wet sidewalk and fell on top of her. She begged him not to hurt her, and his desire was fed by her high, shrill voice and the fear in her huge brown eyes.

He wouldn't remember later what she looked like, whether she was pretty or plain, but he wouldn't forget her eyes, the eyes of a doe caught in the cross hairs of a hunter's bow. He touched her neck with his lips, and she fell silent. There was no sound in the world except the sound of her rapid breathing, in and out, in and out. She seemed to be waiting for Adragon to pierce her flesh, and he felt as if the woman wanted him to take her.

He rolled off and pushed her roughly away from him, ground the side of her face into the sidewalk and made her start to plead again. On his knees, he watched the terrified woman rise and run until she was out of sight. Then somewhere he found the strength to stand and walk away, in the opposite direction from that his near-victim had taken.

Adragon walked until he was back on the main drag, close to where he had secreted the Mustang on a side street hours before. He kept listening for sirens and wondering how good a description she would be able to give them, but the rain had stopped and the streets were quiet except for the sounds of the night people moving past him, communicating in their own private language.

The Mustang was dry and warm but Adragon sat shivering violently for several minutes before he drove back to Del's house. He kept repeating to himself that he was safe, that the girl hadn't gone to the police. He trembled with the pain of denial, and with relief that he was not a murderer.

When he told Del about it, he was surprised at the depth of her anger.

"Adragon, the girl was obviously a prostitute. What were you thinking?"

"I wasn't thinking, Del. I wasn't thinking at all. I was following a primitive urge. I was an animal."

"There was no reason for it. I warned you, I taught you how to control it." Then, "I'm sorry," she relented, and reached to touch his cheek, but he pushed her hand away.

"I should have gone through with it."

"No, you shouldn't have. She could have been diseased. If you had broken the skin—"

"I need it, Del." He was already sorry he had pushed her hand away when she tried to comfort him.

"You have to learn control, Adragon. We're members of a subculture, not very welcome in most corners of the world. If we get careless and expose ourselves to too much public scrutiny, it could mean the end of our kind."

"Help me," he pleaded, and pulled Del down onto the bed beside him. She resisted, trying to reclaim her anger, but he broke her down. She let him pierce her throat, but she forced him to drink slowly and sparingly, to stop before the sweet blood rushing through his veins pushed him beyond her control. He knew that he was capable of hurting her, and he stopped when she put gentle pressure on his chest and slid out from under him.

He opened his eyes but saw only red flames, as if the blood he had consumed covered his eyes. For two or three minutes, he panted heavily and fought the desire to use Del to sate his appetite. Then his eyesight returned, and he realized that his hunger had abated. He sighed and reached for Del, who came readily into his arms.

They made love slowly, as equals, each taking and giving in turn. They bonded and melded so well that Adragon could not tell where one of them ended and the other began. For hours, he was neither male nor female but a perfect blending of the best of both sexes. When they finally rolled apart, their bodies slick with sweat, their mouths full of the taste of each other and the bittersweet taste of blood, Adragon felt as if he had completed a rite of passage.

Despite his satisfaction, Adragon didn't sleep that night. As Del snuggled in his arms, he came to the realization that his life had gotten completely out of control. The vampire game was no longer a game. It was serious business, and he was involved in it up to his neck. He wanted out, and he vowed that he would get out. But one question nagged at him through the long, dark hours of the night: how would he walk away from Del? Where would he get the courage?

The week of Adragon's enforced abstinence from Del's blood was one of the longest weeks of his life, and he spent it roaming the mean streets of his childhood, despite Del's warnings.

It was winter in Asbury Park: the beach deserted, the sand undisturbed by footprints. There weren't many people on the streets. It was cold, and the wind was blowing in freezing sheets off the Atlantic onto First Street. Bruce Springsteen was in California where it was warm, and the local musicians, those Bruce wanna-bes who could afford to, had followed him across the continent to warmer shores. Asbury Park was quiet, except for the blare of juke-boxes and the occasional shout of anger or impatience that escaped through the thin apartment walls of its captive winter residents.

Adragon picked a low-class bar with a dirty plate-glass window and a door that seldom opened to admit or discharge a patron. Occasionally, sound seeped through the door, but no laughter. Where he stood, two or three feet to the right of the door, he could smell the sweat, the urine, the stale beer. A few people drifted by on the sidewalk, but no one stopped to ask him what he was doing there.

He waited less than twenty minutes, not feeling the cold, hot with anticipation. The girl Adragon watched was young for a dive, young and pretty in a sad sort of way. She obviously didn't know she was pretty, or she wouldn't have had to wear the excessive makeup or the skin-tight red skirt that left her shapely legs exposed to the biting wind.

"Hi," Adragon said at exactly the right second, just as she reached out to touch the door but before she had a chance to push it inward.

"Yeah, hi. Do I know you?" The way she squinted her eyes and peered at his face convinced Adragon that she had left her glasses at home and wasn't wearing contacts.

"No, probably not. You don't happen to have a cigarette on you, do you? I really need a drag, and I left mine in the car."

She shook her head indicating that she couldn't supply a smoke and looked him up and down. "What're you doing here? You waiting for someone?"

"Maybe I'm waiting for you."

"Sure you are." She snorted and moved closer; Adragon caught a whiff of perfume, cheap but not unpleasant, and his need multiplied.

"You don't look like you belong around here," she observed, and Adragon hoped that his expensive clothes wouldn't be his undoing.

85

"I came down from New York," he lied. "Somebody told me the Park was a swinging place all year round."

"They lied," she said, then laughed loudly at her own cleverness.

"Damn straight," Adragon agreed, joining in her laughter. "Look, if you're not meeting a guy or something, how about a cup of coffee. On me."

"Coffee? You kidding? Nobody offers a girl coffee around here."

"I just did."

"So you did. Okay, why not?"

Adragon moved away from the wall of the building and offered his arm. After only a moment's hesitation, the girl took it. When he felt the light bird-wing touch of her hand on his arm, he experienced a momentary wave of sadness and shame for what he was about to do to her.

She stopped dead when she focused in on the car Adragon pointed out as his. "A convertible. Why couldn't I have met you in the summertime?"

"I'll be around in the summer." It wasn't a lie; he would be around. Maybe she wouldn't.

"Will you take me for a ride then?"

"Absolutely."

He helped her into the car and closed the door with a solid *thunk*. From his side, he activated the lock that would prevent her from making an easy escape at a stop sign or a traffic light, if she changed her mind about trusting him.

It wasn't hard to convince the girl that walking on the beach in the dead of winter was a romantic thing to do. She appeared to be starved for affection, and Adragon was a good actor. Hidden from the street, he pushed her down on the sand and ripped off her thin jacket. She started to protest when she heard her red sweater tear, but he silenced her with a hand over her mouth.

"Shut up, or you're dead," he threatened, and it thrilled him to realize that he meant it. ". . . or you're dead," he repeated, just to hear the sound of it again.

She struggled feebly but she was no match for Adragon. He was as strong as ten men. As strong as one vampire. The bite he made wasn't much more than a scratch, he was that afraid of hurting her, but it gave up a few drops of her blood, and that was all he had ever had of Del's blood. It was enough to satisfy him, but he knew the time was coming when it would not be enough. He also knew that the girl would be safe tonight, but not in the future.

She was crying, sobbing noisily into her hands, but he pulled them away and made her look at him.

"If you ever see me again, go the other way," he told her. "Don't talk to me, run in the opposite direction. Do you understand?"

She nodded her head and cringed away from him, shaking more from fear than from the biting cold. He stood and pulled his wallet out of the pocket of his jeans. Without looking to see how much he had, he offered it to the girl, stuffed it in the pocket of her jacket when she wouldn't take it from him.

"Don't tell anyone about this," he warned, and she nodded emphatically. He left her there on the beach, to make the long walk back to town in her insufficient clothing, and the human part of him hated the other part, the part that was capable of such inhumanity.

He didn't even realize then that the girl had scratched him. When he leaned on the sink and looked in the steamy bathroom mirror the next morning, he thought the blood was hers, from the shallow cuts he had made on her neck. When they didn't wash off, he knew that they were scratches, probably made when she tried to push his face away from her neck.

Del didn't mention the marks on his face but her attitude changed that day, and she suddenly became more solicitous of Adragon's needs.

"You'll be here tonight, won't you?" she asked over

87

morning coffee. Adragon was sitting at the breakfast table with her for once, unable to sleep due to the vivid memories of what he had done the night before.

"What kind of question is that?" he responded to her inquiry, "I live here now, remember? Why, is something up?"

"I thought we'd have a little party. Would you like that?"

"A party? What's the occasion?"

"We don't need an occasion, do we? I just want to do something nice for you, that's all."

"A party sounds great."

"Fine, I'll leave the shop early and pick up some wine and finger food on my way home."

"Anything I can do to help?"

"You just go back to bed and get some rest. You have circles under your eyes." She kissed him on the cheek and, if it hadn't been for the scratches, the proofs of his betrayal, he would have pulled her into his arms and kissed her the way he wanted to.

Adragon went back to bed after Del left the condo to open her boutique, and slept until late afternoon. When he awoke the second time that day, the events of the preceding evening were less clear in his mind, more easy to accept.

Del, as promised, came home early carrying a brown grocery bag, and asked Adragon to run down to the car and bring up the rest of the party food. He was surprised to find only two additional brown paper bags in the trunk of the red Nissan.

"What's this?" he asked back in the apartment where he set the bags on the kitchen table.

"The stuff for the party," Del answered from the sink. She had her back to him, busy chopping vegetables for a stir-fry dinner.

"Two six packs of wine coolers? Some party."

Del turned from the sink and gave him a jolt with the full wattage of her striking green eyes. "There are two girls coming over, Adragon. They call themselves 'donors,' and they are used to coming here. The wine will be more than sufficient."

"Donors?" he mimicked. "Just what is it these girls 'donate'? Oh, no, not—"

"Blood to vampires," Del finished for him. "Yes, that's exactly what they do."

"You've got to be kidding. You can't just invite somebody over for drinks and then say 'Oh, before you go, how about giving me a pint of your blood, my supply's running low.'"

"They *want* to do this, Adragon. It turns them on."

"Oh, my God." He smacked his forehead with the palms of both hands and started to pace around the kitchen. "I don't want the blood of some stranger, Del, I want your blood."

"Is that an admission that you're a vampire, Adragon?"

He grabbed her by the arms and shook her roughly, the knife she was holding clattered to the floor. He bent over, picked it up, rinsed it off in the sink, and handed it back to her.

"I'm sorry, Del, I didn't mean to hurt you. I'm just not ready to have a friendly chat about vampirism yet."

She nodded and kept her silence for several minutes before she brought the subject up again. "These girls are attractive, Adragon, and clean, and they have no impurities in their blood. We insist that they have two blood tests every month. If the results aren't perfect, we refuse to use them again."

"We?"

"Those of us who use their services."

"The members of the Society?" Elsbeth?

Del shrugged and turned back to the sink, chopped a rib of celery into small pieces before she spoke again.

"I know you'd rather have my blood, Adragon, as I would rather have yours but, as I already explained, we can't always have exactly what we want. Will you get the Wok down for me, please?"

"If you're cooking for me, don't bother."

She laid the knife on the draining board and placed both of her hands on Adragon's shoulders. He could feel their dampness through his shirt, along with the heat he always felt when she touched him.

"You have to eat, Adragon, your vampire nature isn't as strong as your human nature yet. You've been a human for seventeen years, and your diabetes is a part of your physical makeup. If you're not careful, you could become ill and require hospitalization, and that could be very dangerous. Anyway, we all have to eat. For one thing, we have to retain a tolerance for food, to keep up our human facade.

"Hundreds of years ago, when we didn't eat or drink anything but blood, we were too easily singled out and labeled as 'different.' We were white and gaunt, unable to stand the touch of the sunlight on our skin. It has taken us a long time to learn the lessons of survival in a mostly human world, Adragon. Now that you're one of us, you must take advantage of our hard-earned knowledge."

He nodded, mumbled something about needing a shower, and left Del to her dinner preparations. His mind was whirling with contradictory thoughts. He wasn't a vampire, couldn't be a vampire, had attacked a girl less than twenty-four hours ago, and sucked blood from a wound in her neck. The power of suggestion, that's what it was. That's all it was, the power of Del's mind invading his, to suggest the horrible things he actually imagined he had done.

Then why, he asked his reflection in the mirror, why are you trembling with anticipation over the little party Del has planned for you? Are you a vampire, Adragon, or are you really losing it?

Del knocked on the bathroom door to speed him up, and Adragon splashed a little water around before he unlocked the door. After dinner, he dressed in jeans and a T-shirt, and walked into the living room, where Del was adjusting the CD player to exactly the right pitch for a Rod Stewart medley. He was surprised to see that she wore a short red dress with the back cut low to expose her pale flesh. He refused to entertain the nagging thought that there would be something sexual in the nature of Del's relationship with one of the female donors. He averted his eyes, and neither of them spoke until there was a soft rap on the door that led to the elevators.

"Are you okay?" Del asked, and he nodded, the smart retort he had planned stuck in his throat.

Del opened the door before he could find his voice to tell her to stop, and he knew that he had taken one more step on the road to destruction.

Both girls looked younger than Adragon, and they had been carefully chosen. One was a fluffy blonde with a rosy complexion and a ripe body. The other one was lanky, with long, straight hair and soulful eyes. He couldn't have chosen between them, and he didn't have to. Del gave him the blonde, and the girl suited him perfectly. As much as he loved Del, he was hardly aware of the fact that she and the second girl had disappeared from the living room. His mind was devoid of sensible thought, his body pulsed with desires that the blonde could obviously fulfill. That much he could tell just by looking at her, and by letting her look at him.

The girl's blue eyes lingered on every separate inch of Adragon's body, moving upward slowly until her eyes met his. He had expected amusement but he couldn't detect anything but desire in her gaze. "I want you, Adragon," she said, her pouty red lips forming each word slowly and carefully.

He took a step toward her, and she took a step backward, teasing. "Who are you?" he asked.

"You can call me Verna," she answered in her practiced,

sultry voice. It wasn't the answer to his question, but it would do.

"Verna, from vernal? A dew-wet blade of vernal grass."

"What's that? Did you write that?"

"I think so." They were stepping together toward the white couch, the same white couch where he had first touched Del. He ran the back of his hand down the girl's cheek, her neck, let his fingers drop to the solid young flesh of her shoulder. She sank to the couch and pulled him beside her, but when he tried to kiss her, she turned her head away.

"That's one of the rules," she intoned, as if she had made the same statement a hundred times before, to a hundred different men, "no kissing." "Okay," he agreed, not really caring, "no kissing." The girl's hands moved over Adragon's body expertly, and he became more aroused by the minute.

"If there are rules, you must already know what I want," he mumbled against her neck where his tongue was drawing intricate patterns on her rosy skin.

In answer, she arched away from him and brushed her golden hair behind her ear. Adragon stared at the tracery of veins in her throat, saw them pulse with life, saw the girl lick her lips in anticipation of the act he would perform, more intimate than a love-sex act, more deadly than rough sex.

"Are you ready?" she asked. Her lips had become the color of blood, and Adragon couldn't hold back. He threw himself down on top of her and ripped at her neck with his teeth. She cried out something that Adragon couldn't make out, and he reached up to cover her mouth with his right hand, tangling his left in her hair to hold her head steady.

"Stop," the girl managed to mumble, and Adragon pressed his hand harder across her mouth.

"You asked for this," he hissed in her ear. "This is

what you came for, this is what turns you on, isn't it?"

She tried to shake her head but Adragon jerked on her hair until she stopped struggling. His sharp incisors punctured a vein, and Verna's blood spurted into Adragon's face. The smell of the fresh blood assaulted his nostrils, and his thirst was suddenly overwhelming. He buried his face in the girl's neck and swallowed a large amount of blood before the reality of what he was doing struck him and stopped him cold.

He applied pressure on the wound in the now silent girl's throat, but her blood kept flowing, a sticky, red stream that he knew was emptying her body of its life force. Her eyes were closed, her arms limp.

"Wake up," he commanded, using his free hand to slap her face. "I need some water," he mumbled. Then, loud enough to wake the dead, "Del, I need some water. Bring me some water, damn it!"

He tried to prop the girl up on the couch, but she slid down, and his hand slipped off her neck. A handful of bright red blood splashed onto the white couch, crimson flowers bloomed on the white carpet.

"Del . . ." he shouted, and she came into the room naked, the slim brunet trailing behind her.

"I don't know what happened, Del, I think she's dead, my God what will we do if she's dead, I think I killed her." He was hysterical, screaming and crying, tears streaming down his cheeks and into his mouth. He wiped at his eyes and smeared his face with the girl's blood, tasted its bitterness on his tongue when he licked his lips.

"She isn't dead, Adragon," Del said calmly, gazing down into Verna's white face, "but she will be if you don't get hold of yourself."

"Holy Christ," the girl behind her mumbled, "doesn't he know anything about being a vampire?"

Chapter Ten

"Get down on your knees," Del instructed, and gave Adragon a push to help him along. "Now bend over her, put your mouth on her throat, over the wound."

"I can't," he whimpered, feeling bile rise in his throat and threaten to bring up his stir-fry vegetables. "I can't, Del."

"You have to." Del had a good grip on the back of his neck and she pushed his head down until his lips touched the girl's bloody throat. "Do you want to let her die, Adragon?"

"No, I can't let her die, I can't."

"Then put your mouth on the wound. You don't have to suck her blood, just lick your lips and rub them back and forth across the broken skin. That's it," she said when he started to follow her instructions, "just a little longer. Let me see the wound now."

Adragon pulled his head back so that he wouldn't be blocking Del's line of vision. When he got up the nerve to look at Verna's neck, he thought that his eyes were deceiving him. There was a lot of dried blood, and some wet blood in the immediate vicinity of the wound, but there was no fresh flow. The wound had stopped bleeding.

"Did I do that?" he asked wonderingly. "Did I stop the bleeding?"

"You fucked up, Del," the long-haired girl accused, ignoring Adragon. "He was supposed to know all this stuff before he used one of us. Poor Verna." The girl stared down at her friend, who appeared to be in a deep sleep. Her yellow-blond hair was wet with perspiration, and it was matted to her pasty skin. She was no longer the healthy-looking girl that Del had admitted to the condo only a short time ago.

"Shut up, Rox, Verna will be fine," Del said quickly, shooting Adragon a look, "and she'll be paid handsomely for her inconvenience."

"Is that what you call it, almost dying because of him?"

"I want you to forget what you saw here tonight," Del told the girl, turning to look her in the eye. "I don't ever want to hear it mentioned again, do you understand me?"

"Sure," Rox answered nervously, unable to stand up to Del's steady gaze. "Good," Del said, "now get dressed. As soon as Verna's feeling better, I'll send you home in a cab."

It wasn't until the girls had been tucked into the back seat of a taxicab driven by a friend of Del's that she turned on Adragon. "That was really stupid. I told you that our saliva can stop bleeding, but only if the wound is one we made ourselves."

"I panicked, I forgot everything when I saw all that blood. God, I thought I'd killed her."

"You almost did. But that's not what really troubles me."

"If murder doesn't trouble you, what does?"

"Save your sarcasm, Adragon. The girl lost a great deal of blood. Rox is going to be watching her carefully, and a member of the Society who has medical training will drop in on her later."

"So, what's the problem? This person should be able to give her a transfusion, right?"

"Give her a transfusion of whose blood, Adragon?"

"I don't get it."

95

"We're all vampires, my darling, with vampire blood flowing through our veins."

Adragon's face changed as the horror of what she was saying dawned on him.

"No," he protested, "I don't believe it. If you gave Verna a transfusion of vampire blood, she'd turn into a vampire?"

"I can only say for sure that it would start a process, put an irreversible current in motion."

"Well, look on the bright side, maybe Verna would *like* being a vampire."

Adragon wasn't surprised that Del locked her bedroom door while he was still on the other side of it. He lay down on the rumpled sheets in the guest room, and didn't wake up when Del's alarm went off the next morning. He finally saw her again at dinnertime, and it was obvious from the stiff way she greeted him that she was still irritated with him.

"Did you hear anything about the girl?" he asked from his perch on a high kitchen stool.

Del was unpacking a bag from the deli, arranging ham and cheese on Chinette plates. "Her name is Verna, in case you've forgotten, and she's doing all right, still weak but improving."

"No transfusion?"

"No transfusion necessary."

"I'm sorry about last night, Del." Adragon slid off the stool and tried to pull her into his arms, but Del pushed him away.

"I don't like your attitude, Adragon," she told him, and he felt a twinge of real fear. What if she was more angry than he'd thought, what if she was really disgusted with him, what if she wanted him to move out?

"What attitude?" he asked with more bravado than he felt. "I said I'm sorry, what else do you want me to do?"

"I want you to grow up, Adragon," she answered quietly, "I want you to start taking your responsibilities seriously."

"Okay, I will. You're right, I will." Del smiled and Adragon pulled her into his arms, and this time she didn't try to resist him. Her body seemed to lose its own form and become one with his, to fill every empty spot, to make him a complete person.

"Let's eat later," he suggested, "you don't want food, do you?"

She shook her head and placed her hungry mouth on his. In the middle of their kiss, he remembered to ask her a question. "Why no kissing?" he asked on the way to the bedroom. "Verna told me 'no kissing,' " he explained when Del didn't seem to understand his question.

"You tried to kiss her?"

"I was caught up in the moment, it wasn't as if I really wanted to kiss her. Answer the question, will you?"

"Isn't it obvious? They're afraid it's contagious."

"Contagious? Oh God!" Adragon started to laugh hysterically, and it was easy for Del to push him down to the bed and remove his jeans. She straddled him, and leaned down to nibble on his neck.

"I can't believe it," he told her minutes later, "I honest to God can't believe that those blood groupies are afraid they'll catch vampirism through kissing."

Talking about the donors reminded Adragon of something else he wanted to ask Del. "You said something last night about 'compensating' the girl — excuse me, Verna. If you'll tell me how to take care of it, I'll send her something tomorrow."

"Don't worry about it," Del answered, as she slid her sleek body into the silky green robe that Adragon loved. "Let's have some dinner now, okay? I'm starving."

"I want to worry about it, Del. Verna sure as hell deserves something for her trouble, don't you think?"

"I've already taken care of it." Del walked away, toward

the kitchen, and Adragon followed hot on her heels, his breath coming in short little gasps.

"You've taken care of it?" he asked, as he caught up to her and grabbed her arm, whirling her around. "You've taken care of it? What does that make you, my pimp? Or maybe you're *her* pimp. I'm confused, Del, help me out here, will you?"

"You're a vampire, Adragon, and if you don't want to end up with a stake through your heart, you'd better start showing some sense, and following the rules."

"I am not a vampire," he yelled at the top of his lungs. "Don't say that. I forbid you to say that." He shook her with all his strength, trying to hurt her, but her body went limp and she laughed softly.

"Look in the mirror, little boy," she whispered. She tugged him back toward the bedroom, to a full-length mirror that stood in a silver frame at the end of her bed. She adjusted it, pushed the top of it backward so that he could see his image, then she waited, still smiling.

Reluctantly, he pulled his gaze away from her face. He looked into the mirror, against his will, with no desire to discover what the beautiful woman who stood beside him saw in his face. What he saw there shocked him, stunned him. He pushed Del away from him and concentrated his full attention on the reflection in the glass.

He was taller, his arms and legs longer, his chest more muscular. He looked strong, strong and dangerous. His complexion was ruddy, his eyes deep, dark pools which didn't seem to reflect the light in the room. Del had touched a switch that flooded the room with light, but none of it reached his eyes. He wondered if this was what the girls in Asbury Park had seen, what the other girl, Verna, had seen last night. If it was, why hadn't they been more frightened, more leery of letting him touch them? He looked as if he were . . .

"Why?" he asked Del, but his eyes remained on his own

reflection. "Why did you do this to me?" When he turned to her, he could see that she was frightened.

"It's been coming for weeks, Adragon, you knew that. Don't pretend that you didn't know what was happening to you. It's complete now, the transformation is complete."

"Why, Del, why now?" He was screaming inside, so calm on the outside that Del was wary.

"Because of the amount of blood you consumed last night. It happened too fast, it should have been a more gradual process."

He turned swiftly, and Del took a clumsy step backward. "I didn't do anything to you, Adragon, you were born to this, it's always been there, under the surface, more real than your humanness."

"Go away." It wasn't a request, but she stayed, searching his face, as if she were looking for a familiar landmark.

"Don't close me out, Adragon," she said finally. "It's important that we talk about this."

"Go away, damn it. Go away and leave me alone."

Del started to protest, then thought better of it. When he was alone in the room, he bolted the bedroom door, then removed his clothing and stood naked before the mirror, the bright light from the ceiling fixture touching every inch of his firm young skin, his tousled dark hair. He had never before admired himself that way, flexed his muscles and watched the play of light ripple down his arms, across his chest. He was a man now, not just an extension of Elsbeth, and the mere thought of his manhood sent a wave of desire pounding through his body.

"I'm beautiful," he told his image, "I am — " But he couldn't finish the thought or find the words he needed to speak aloud. He opened the sliding glass doors and sat on the balcony for hours, with the freezing wind off the ocean caressing his naked body with icy fingers. He didn't feel the cold. He felt the power and the mystery, the destiny that pulled him forward. "I am . . ."

Sometime toward morning, Adragon stepped back into Del's bedroom and found it empty. He took his leather jacket from the hall closet and moved silently past the door to the guest bedroom. He could sense that she was in there, awake, watching the patterns projected on the ceiling by the light she had left burning, so that he could see his way, in case he desired to go to her in the night.

"Where are you going, Adragon?" The question came out of nowhere, and he knew that Del had projected it into his mind without the need for words. There was no way that he could have answered her.

Adragon drove straight to the street where Elsbeth lived, drove past the house, and parked several blocks away, on the street in front of a house that was surrounded by a high wall. He knew that his car would go undetected, unsuspected, for hours.

He trudged across the sand and walked north, toward the huge ultra-modern showplace which his mother's horrific prose had built for them. The house was dark and quiet, with only two windows lit from within. There was a dim light in Elsbeth's quarters and another in the room where Adragon had spent the last several years of his life, since they had so effortlessly slipped from the poverty level to upper middle class. He felt a stab of anger as he wondered what his mother was doing in his room. He envisioned her picking up his belongings, filling boxes with his books, his pewter collection, his sweaters, the model planes he had glued together with his own shaky adolescent hands.

Or maybe she wasn't packing. Maybe she was ripping pages from his precious books, or scratching his CDs and unraveling his tapes.

He pushed the offending images to the back of his mind and dropped to his knees in the wet sand. He noticed his discomfort for the first minutes; after that, his mind flew to Elsbeth's room and found her there. The light in his room was burning to welcome him in from the darkness; he had misjudged his mother. His mind met hers and they melded. He read her thoughts and shared her visions, her memories, her love. She wasn't angry, as he had expected her to be. She was hurt, in pain because he had left her. She had been calling to him, sending out messages, beseeching him to come back to her. She knew that he was close now. She saw him squatting in the sand, the tide washing over his sneakers, his feet turning blue with cold.

His mind fought the control she exerted, wrestled free from the clutching tendrils of thought that snaked from her mind to his. Finally, he stood and walked back to his car, oblivious of the below freezing temperature. Once he stopped and looked back at his mother's house. "I hate you, Elsbeth," he shouted into the wind. "Do you hear me? I hate you, and I won't come back to you. Not ever."

He slept in the bed with Del for what was left of the night, and she wanted him to make love to her but he couldn't. He was physically and mentally exhausted, capable of nothing more than holding her in his arms and inhaling the sweet, fresh scent of her body that mingled with the acrid smell of her blood. He could smell her blood through her skin, hear it pulsing in her veins, taste it on his tongue without ever touching her. But the longing was there, and it was strong, almost too much for him to handle. He had changed since he drank the bitter blood of the girl, Verna, and he felt as if she had given him something bad that he was never going to be able to purge from his body.

Del patted him and held him in her arms, his curly head pressed to her silken breast. He slept, and woke several times in the night to pull her closer, to angrily deny his fate and cry out into the black abyss for a savior.

101

Chapter Eleven

When he awoke at noon, Adragon was still shaken by what he had learned about himself the night before. How, he wondered, did you go about ridding yourself of unwanted vampire tendencies? Could you successfully reverse the process once it was set in motion? Was there an antidote for the poisonous effects of vampirism on your body and soul? Was it all in his head, or wasn't it?

He was also shaken by the enormity of his feelings toward his mother, the love and hate, the respect and disgust that constantly vied for control of his emotions. He had shouted into the night that he hated his mother but that statement was only as true as his state of mind was stable at the moment he had made it. Adragon had always loved his mother; they had been best friends for as long as he could remember. How could he say that he hated her now, without proclaiming that he loved her with his next breath? What was the rift between them about anyway, the fact that she had joined the Society of Vampires without him?

Adragon poured himself a second cup of coffee from the pot that Del had left for him. Although it was Sunday, she had opened the small boutique she owned and operated, something about a "special sale." Adragon was alone in the sterile white condo, longing for the companionship of even a dog or a cat, impossible since Del was allergic to both.

He had just spread the sports section of the *Asbury Park Press* out on the counter beside the coffeepot when the telephone rang. For a moment, he thought of ignoring it, then decided that it might be Del calling to tell him that she would be home early. He picked it up, his "hello" sounding too loud to his own ears in the silent kitchen.

"Adragon? Are you alone?"

"Yeah."

There was a long silence on the line, and he smiled, hoping that he was making her uncomfortable.

"Are you all right?"

"Sure." He wondered how long he could get away with the one-word answers before she jumped all over him.

"Are you taking your medicine?"

"Yeah, Ray brought it over, remember?"

"Your medical condition is very serious, Adragon, I worry about you."

"I know you do, Mother, and I appreciate it."

"You can always come home, Adragon," she said after a lengthy pause, "you know that."

"I know," he admitted.

"I was thinking about you last night, feeling that you were close to me, wishing that we could sit down and talk like we used to. Remember our all-night gab sessions?"

He didn't answer. She knew that he was there last night, so close. She knew.

"I love you, Adragon."

"Me, too."

"Do you?"

"Elsbeth—"

The line was dead, and he had tears in his eyes, tears that Del would never have understood.

The next evening, Del came home late, loaded down

103

with shopping bags filled with gifts. She placed them on a shelf in the hall closet and threatened Adragon with bodily harm if he dared to touch their bright, metallic wrappings. In spite of the decorations on the streets and the ads on TV, he had forgotten that it was only a few days before Christmas. He cleaned out his savings account to buy a gift for Del, a necklace with stones that matched her eyes. He didn't buy a gift for Elsbeth and when one arrived from her, he put it in a dresser drawer, unopened. He meant to telephone her on Christmas Eve but it didn't happen, and Del's phone was silent. They decorated a small tree, and Del gave him a signed first edition of *The Stand*. They made wild love, "vampire love" she called it, high on spiked eggnog and the taste of each other's blood, and Adragon slept away half of what had always been his favorite holiday.

It was several mornings later when the phone woke him, Del was absent from the bed, and he remembered that Christmas had come and gone. The new year was upon him.

"Yeah?" he growled into the phone, damning the person whose idea it had been to place telephones on nightstands, within easy reach of sleepers.

"Adragon? That doesn't sound like you, my boy. Voice deepening, is it?" It was Raymond Sadler's deep, resonant voice that interrupted Adragon's musings.

"It's me alright, Ray, what can I do for you?"

"Well, since you put it so bluntly, I'm afraid your mother is rather upset. It seems that you neglected to get in touch with her over the holiday. She was rather expecting—"

"She should learn not to expect anything," Adragon cut in. "Tell her that, will you?"

"If I may be so bold, what is this love/hate thing you have with Elsbeth?"

"I love the woman, Ray, I just don't like her."

104

"That's a rather nasty thing for a boy your age to say about his mother."

"Yeah, you're right. I'm sorry. I'll call her tonight, okay? I'll tell her I was confused and didn't know what day it was."

"No need to be sarcastic, my boy. Actually, I was ringing you up for another reason."

"What's up, Ray?"

"I thought we might go to lunch tomorrow, my treat, of course."

"Sure, why not?" Raymond was obviously planning to deliver a sermon, but Adragon thought he might as well get it over and done with.

"I can meet you somewhere, or pick you up at Miss Keelan's condo."

"Just name the place and I'll meet you there."

Raymond named a popular seafood restaurant on the shore, set a time, and hung up quickly, without any further mention of Elsbeth. Adragon didn't say anything to Del about Raymond's call. He decided that since Ray, Del, and Elsbeth all seemed to enjoy their little intrigues so thoroughly, he would spend some time playing them one against the other in an effort toward discovering just what it was about their nasty games that gave them so much pleasure.

Noon the following day found Adragon damp from his shower, shoving his legs into a pair of navy dress pants and hunting for a cranberry sweater he was sure he had stuffed into his bag the night he left Elsbeth's house. He ran a comb through his hair and left the condo quickly, only to arrive at the restaurant early. He sat slouched behind the wheel of the Mustang until the older man's gray Lincoln edged into the parking lot and pulled up beside him. Adragon stepped out of his car and waited as Raymond carefully locked the big silvery-gray car and walked around the front of it. He greeted Adragon warmly, and threw his arm around the boy's shoulders, as if they were old friends.

"Adragon, my boy, you're looking well."

"Hi, Ray, nice to see you. You, too."

Adragon couldn't help but wonder what the hell they would talk about over lunch. Why had he so readily accepted the man's invitation? He followed Ray into the restaurant and sat down across from him in a comfortable booth, dreading the time that stretched out in front of him, but his lunch partner was all smiles.

"I hope this is satisfactory. I remembered that you favor seafood."

"Yeah, this is great, thanks for inviting me."

"Elsbeth is so concerned about your diet. When she learned that I was taking you to lunch—"

"You told her?"

"I'm sorry. Should I have kept it a secret?"

Adragon shook his head and bit his tongue to keep from saying the first thing that had slipped into his mind. So, Ray was on a mission for Elsbeth. Adragon wondered if his mother was picking up the tab, or if it was truly Raymond's treat.

"So," the man began after they had placed their orders, "how do you like your new living arrangements?"

"Ray, I don't think you and I should discuss my relationship with Del Keelan. If my mother wants information, she can call me herself."

"I'm afraid you've misinterpreted my motives, my boy. When your mother mentioned to me that you were no longer living at home, I became concerned about your welfare. I realize that this may be a touchy subject, but if there's anything I can do monetarily?"

"I'm fine," Adragon had to lie, since he had no money of his own at all since buying Del's Christmas gift.

"Oh, here are the salads. Should you be eating blue cheese? Sorry, I am first and foremost a doctor, you know.

Which reminds me to ask if you have a physician to assist you in monitoring your blood glucose levels?"

"Elsbeth and I have done that on our own for years, Ray. Anyway, I feel great, I never felt better."

Raymond placed his salad fork on the half-empty plate and pushed it away from him. "I promised your mother that I'd either get you to a doctor or take a blood sample myself. People who have juvenile diabetes—"

Adragon slammed his right arm down hard on the table, palm upward, rattling the salad plates and water glasses. "Here, Ray, go ahead and draw a little blood. I hope none of these people who're staring at us are squeamish, because I tend to be a bleeder, but don't let that stop you."

"Please, Adragon . . ."

"Don't 'please' me, Ray, you're here as my mother's watchdog, aren't you? Taking time out of your busy life to keep Elsbeth happy? Tell me, what's in it for you, Ray?"

Raymond did the most frightening thing that he could have done then, short of producing a needle and drawing blood right there at the table. He placed his soft hand with its well-manicured nails on top of Adragon's hand and squeezed it intimately.

"What in the hell are you up to, Ray?" Adragon asked after he had pulled his hand away and hidden it in his lap. Ray didn't answer, and Adragon finally took a deep breath, straightened the plates and glasses, and apologized for his outburst. Raymond smilingly motioned to their waitress, who was hovering a couple of booths away, waiting to be summoned. Their lunch was only slightly warm when they received it, but it didn't matter. Even though he had eaten very little breakfast, Adragon had lost his appetite somewhere along the way.

After that, Raymond discussed the weather and then local politics, about which Adragon knew practically nothing, but the subject helped pass the time through

107

their fish and baked potatoes, to the cup of black coffee Ray always drank after a meal.

On the way back to their cars, Ray once again brought up the subject of his interference in Adragon's life.

"I have no quarrel with you, my boy, believe me. I've tried to be a good friend to your mother, and a responsible person myself."

"Okay, the blood test would be a good idea. I'll go along with it, I'll be adult about it. Do you want me to come over to your house, or what?" As long as he'd known Raymond, which had been for several years, Adragon had never visited his office or had any medical services performed by him. As far as Adragon knew, the man's friendship with Elsbeth had never crossed over onto a professional level either, although Elsbeth had been a nurse before her son was born and continued to work as an LPN when he was a toddler.

"That won't be necessary," Raymond answered smiling broadly, "we can take care of it in my car, in the parking lot. I always carry my bag with me, in case of an emergency. Once a doctor —"

"Sure," Adragon answered shortly, "but isn't this a bad time to take blood, right after I've eaten a big meal? Elsbeth usually took it the first thing in the morning, before I had my breakfast."

"You're absolutely right, Adragon, most doctors prefer a fasting blood sugar when they're monitoring a diabetic. But to expedite matters, I'll take your blood now and attempt to compensate for your recent caloric intake when I calculate your sugar level."

Short minutes later, Adragon sat in the front passenger seat of the silver Lincoln while Raymond pulled a syringe from his bag and poked at the boy's inner arm, searching for a prominent vein. When he found one, he dabbed at the skin with an alcohol wipe and plunged the needle painlessly into the vein.

108

Adragon sat with his eyes closed and his hands clenched, not because the blood-letting ritual bothered him — it didn't. But the situation was so damned incongruous. Young, well-dressed professional people with perfectly coiffed hair had walked out of the restaurant with Ray and Adragon. They crossed the parking lot laughing, flirting, putting together business deals that would help them make this month's exorbitant payments on their Datsuns or Toyotas. Inside the restaurant, several older couples lingered over their coffee, while one or two younger couples leaned close to each other across the tables. And Adragon sat in a car in the parking lot giving what seemed to be a ridiculous amount of his blood to a doctor who didn't even have an office, so far as he knew.

After Raymond drove away, Adragon sat in the parking lot and watched the parade of people for several minutes. Then he drove down to Island Beach State Park and walked up and down in the sand until the pale orange ball that was the winter sun sank into the choppy sea. The waves strained upward to welcome the sun, and the horizon became a rainbow blend of watered-down colors. Adragon didn't leave until the sky was dark, the sun rising somewhere else, on a different horizon.

Del wasn't home but there was a message on the answering machine, "Hi, love, I'll be a little late tonight. I'm sure you can find something to munch on until I get home. Miss me."

When she finally got home around nine, every light in the condo was burning. It didn't take her long to find Adragon. She stopped in the bedroom door and stared at his body, which was as naked as a newborn babe's. He was beautiful, still more boy than man, but matured since the day she met him two months before.

"Do you think someone who hadn't seen me every day for the past month wouldn't notice the change?" he asked.

But he continued to stare at himself, without turning to look at her while she pondered her answer.

"No," she answered finally. "I've seen you every day and I can see the change. You're taller, stronger, you suddenly have facial hair and body hair. I've told you this before."

"I had lunch with an old friend today. No one you know," he hastened to add, "and he acted as if I were the same old Adragon, nothing changed, nothing new."

"Maybe he was afraid of offending you."

Adragon laughed and Del's eyes watched him closely, warily.

"Adragon, can we talk about this? Put your clothes on, and come to the kitchen with me. I'll make some tea, and we'll talk."

"I don't want to talk tonight, Del. As a matter of fact, I may never want to talk again. Do you like what you see?" He caught her eyes in the mirror and held them; she was pinned to the frame of the door, unable to move until he released her. "Because you did this to me, Del," he finished, "so you sure as hell had better like it."

When he broke eye contact with her to stare into his own eyes again, Del turned quickly and moved out of the bedroom, out of range of his mesmerism. He called out to her as she walked quickly down the hallway toward the kitchen. "We'll talk tomorrow, Del, I promise we'll talk tomorrow."

Chapter Twelve

An hour later, Adragon left the condo, although Del begged him not to go.

"You don't know what you're doing, Adragon," she warned, "there are all kinds of dangers."

"We'll talk tomorrow," he promised again when she tried to restrain him. Then he mumbled "thirst," and Del panicked.

"Let me feed you," she begged, "let me take care of you."

But he broke free of her hands and ran from the condo, afraid of the awful thirst and of what he might do to her if he stayed. In the end, he walked the cold, hard-packed sand for hours before returning home to sleep in Del's bed, to feed on her sweet blood. He walked alone, after scavenging the streets of Asbury Park and following a drunken man for a long time, desiring his blood, fearing its impurities that could lead to disease or death.

He walked past the bar where he had picked up the young woman several nights earlier, hoping and fearing that he would catch sight of her. He had worried ever since leaving her on the beach that she had memorized his license number and notified the police of what he had done to her. "He bit my neck, officer, he drank my blood." Not likely, but even the remote possibility that she would report the incident was a cause for uneasiness.

He awoke in a cold sweat, savagely kicking back the

bed covers, fighting down the nausea that rose in his throat.

"I am a vampire," he whispered hoarsely, and Del tossed fitfully and rolled into the warm space he had just vacated.

The room was cold, and that helped clear his head faster. Still, he went into the bathroom, urinated, and sat down on the closed toilet seat for several minutes. It took a long time for his body to stop trembling, his head to stop pounding. The dream had been so damned real, like the nightmares he'd had when he was a little kid, when he'd cried out for Elsbeth to come and hold him, until the sun rose to hide the darkness of the night.

If he hadn't known better, he would have sworn that he had been there, inside the dream. But that was impossible; he remembered coming home to Del, using the tiny razor-sharp instrument to slit her fingers, sucking blood from them until she drew her hand away and slipped it under her pillow, out of his reach.

Anyway, he was warm and dry, except for the sweat that stood on his forehead. In the dream he had been dripping icy water from his hair and shoulders, soaked through to the skin in the cold December rain that was falling outside the windows of the condo, just as it had fallen in the dream. Elsbeth believed in prophetic dreams. Could this have been one?

He had been in Asbury Park, just as he had been, in reality, earlier last night. He recognized the streets, the storefronts, the particular atmosphere that he had discovered nowhere else. Although the streets had remained nameless, he knew that he could find them if he went there again, to that place where — He broke off the thought, unable to accept it fully into his mind.

Say it, Adragon, he urged himself, as the trembling in his hands resumed and spread to his arms and legs. Admit that you dreamed of killing, of the ultimate vampire

112

act. Admit that you enjoyed it, that one part of your being glorified in it, while another part of you was horrified.

He lay down beside Del and she rolled into his arms. Still, the sensation of having satisfied his basest needs and lost his last shred of humanity remained with him for hours. For a minute or so, he wished that none of the events of the past two months had happened, that he could have the power to wipe the slate clean and start again. That there would be no Society of Vampires, no argument with Elsbeth, no Del Keelan. Then the gorgeous, flesh and blood woman snuggled against him and he cursed himself for the thoughts he had been entertaining.

"I never had a choice," he whispered into Del's strawberry-scented hair and she, still sleeping, mumbled her own endearments to him, as he relived the dream.

In Asbury Park, the streets were rain-slick, slippery with the oil and grease droppings from the hundreds of cars that prowled them daily. Adragon was walking, the Mustang nowhere in sight. Maybe a vampire's dreams weren't supposed to include sleek, shining automobiles of the nineties' variety. A vampire's dream: primitive, frightening, rising from a deep, dark level of the subconscious forever closed to mortal man.

The vampire boy (ME, Adragon shouted silently) hid in a recessed doorway and waited for a victim. He wasn't particular, and there was no need to search one out. He knew that someone would come, and that as long as blood flowed in his or her veins, that would be sufficient to satisfy the need, the lust.

The vampire boy heard footsteps, his muscles tightened, he prepared to spring. Shuffling footsteps — someone very old? That prospect was not appealing but the vampire knew that he wouldn't hesitate. His need was too great, he had waited too long. He stood without moving or breathing while the walker slowly approached his hiding place.

He sprang, and almost recoiled in shock. His victim was a child, a young boy, no more than twelve or thirteen, dragging his feet, staring down at them. The vampire thought of asking him what he was doing out alone after dark but, of course, he didn't. The boy's dark eyes clouded with fear when he saw his awful fate leap out of the shadows. But there was a twist to his lips, a tiny half-smile that he refused to surrender, even at the end. "So this is it," he seemed to be thinking, and the vampire admired him for that.

The young boy cried out, one short, sharp burst of pain when his jugular was pierced. Then he gave himself up to the satisfaction of the vampire's desires, as though that was his reason for existing, as if he had always known that Adragon would come for him. He dropped limply to the wet sidewalk, his blood reddening the deep puddles that stood in the broken concrete.

The vampire rose, a boy no more. His incisors were long and pointed, and thick glops of blood dripped from his bearded chin. His shirt and his hands were red with the oozing life of his young victim, and the smile on his handsome, callous face drove fear to the heart of Adragon Hart, the dreamer.

When Del woke up, they made love, slowly and sweetly. Sometimes when Del was like this, Adragon wondered how great her need for blood could be, since she seemed to have no desire to make vampire love. Afterward, she went to the kitchen for coffee. It was still early, and she had plenty of time to get to the boutique before it was time to open.

Adragon wanted to talk, and Del let him.

"I have such power, Del," he told her excitedly. "I can feel my blood rushing through my veins. I think my heart is beating faster. I'm stronger. I feel . . ." He searched for

114

a word, and Del watched him with a smile on her face, as if she knew exactly the phrase he was searching for. "Invincible," he finished, "I feel absolutely invincible. Have you ever felt that way?"

"Your words describe perfectly the way all vampires feel, Adragon, although I realize that males have more physical strength than females, and more need for physical expression. But you haven't even begun to tap the source of your power, you have so much ahead of you, so many wonderful experiences. In a way, I actually envy you this beginning, this new understanding of your origins."

"My origins . . . what are my origins, Del?"

The question seemed to fluster her, to disturb the calm that always surrounded her. "I meant your vampire origins, that you are now a vampire in the great tradition of vampires, carried down through the centuries for thousands of years."

"Is that what you meant?"

"I said it was."

"The last time we spoke about vampirism, you said something about my parents, do you remember that?"

"No." She turned away from him, stacked coffee cups and saucers on the tray she had carried into the bedroom.

"Put that down until we're finished here."

"We are finished."

He put two fingers on her wrist and exerted the smallest bit of pressure until she flinched and dropped the tray onto the bed.

"Are my human origins important, Del?"

"No, they're not."

"Then why did you bring the subject up?" Del shrugged and Adragon's hand shot out, grabbing hold of her arm with such speed and force that she whimpered and tried to pry his fingers off with her free hand.

"Sit still, Del, and tell me what I should know about my

parents and their part in my vampirism, if there really is such a thing."

Del relaxed and Adragon dropped her arm, then settled back against the pillows to hear what he knew she would tell him.

"First of all, you must completely accept the fact that you are a vampire. I can tell that you still think it's some kind of a game, or a trick someone has played on you. As long as you feel that way, you won't feel compelled to learn our ways, and you won't be able to protect yourself from the ways of the world."

"My parents, Del."

She sighed deeply, and rubbed at her forehead with her open hand before she went on. "One of your parents is a vampire, Adragon."

He laughed so long and so hard that Del was able to slip away to the bathroom for several minutes. When he realized that she was gone, he pounded on the door, then opened it and entered. She was in the shower; he could see the outline of her perfect body through the glass shower door. He picked up her towel and waited until she turned the water off.

When she opened the door, he held up the towel, and she nearly fainted with fright.

"You startled me, Adragon. Why did you follow me to the bathroom, what do you want from me?"

"One of my parents is a vampire?"

"I didn't make the rules, and I shouldn't have told you so soon. I'm sorry."

He wrapped the large bath sheet around Del's slender body and guided her back to the bedroom, where he sat her down on the edge of the bed.

"You did this to me, Del. Are you trying to tell me that you couldn't have done it unless there was already vampire blood flowing in my veins?"

She nodded, but he needed much more and he waited

116

patiently for her to explain.

"I was the catalyst but you can't thank me, and you can't blame me. Either you were a vampire before, in a past life, or—"

"Oh, Jesus Christ, spare me!" he groaned.

"It's true, and I think you know it is. Either that, or one of your parents is a vampire, and for some reason they hid your heritage from you, so that you would remain mortal."

"Why would they do that?"

"I don't know, maybe you were being punished for something you did in your last incarnation."

Adragon laughed again, but this time there was an edge to his laughter. "I can't believe that you'd try to feed me a line of crap like that. I thought you said we'd always be honest with each other?"

"I am being honest with you, sweet Adragon, I'm trying to tell you the truth, but it isn't easy. I know it's difficult to believe, that it goes against the grain of everything you've learned about the world of mortals."

"The world of mortals—what a catchy phrase."

"Please be serious, there's so much for you to learn."

"You keep saying that, but you aren't trying to teach me much. What about sunlight? If I'm a vampire, why doesn't sunlight bother me?"

"That myth is a holdover from hundreds of years ago, Adragon. We had to adapt to life in the world of men. Otherwise, we would be hunted down and killed like animals."

"My reflection in the mirror?"

"I'm sure I have always been able to see myself in a looking glass. There is just no basis for that rumor."

"Garlic? Silver bullets? Wooden stakes through the heart?"

"Vampires are not repelled by garlic, and they generally die either by fire or by their own desire to give up their mortal lives and go back into the void. If someone started to drive a stake through your heart, I think the sensible thing to do would be to surrender your life. Vampires are not incapable of feeling pain."

Of course not. He remembered the pain on her face when he had used his newfound strength to squeeze her wrist just minutes ago.

"Do you believe in this," he asked hesitantly, "this dying and living again?"

"I have experienced it, Adragon, for hundreds of years."

"You can remember other lives?" His heart was beating double time, waiting for her answer.

"Only snatches here and there, moments of *déjà vu,* but I know it's true."

"I can't remember anything. If everything you've told me is true, and I'm not saying that it is yet, then why can't I remember?"

"I don't know. I wish I could help you, but I truly don't know the answer."

"Did you know I was . . . what I am when you met me?"

"The first moment I laid eyes on you, I knew that you were an uninitiated vampire. That's just one of the reasons why I wanted you so badly."

"Something like a guy finding a virgin, huh?" he asked.

"Something like that, yes." She smiled and leaned forward to kiss him on the cheek. When she moved back, he had taken her towel and was reaching for one of her exquisite breasts. She took the initiative and he let her make love to him, repressing his desire to be the aggressor. But his heart wasn't in it, and his performance wasn't up to par. All he could think about while Del moved above him was that one of his parents was a vampire, and that he would have to find a way to force Elsbeth into telling him that either she or his father had betrayed him.

118

Chapter Thirteen

Adragon took the back steps two at a time, and pounded on the door with all the pent-up anger he carried with him. This deck faced the ocean, and the wind bit into his legs through his blue jeans and tousled his hair as he waited for his mother to open the door. He was on the eastern side of the big house, where the long narrow deck stretched the length of the living/dining area.

It was nine o'clock in the morning, and he knew that Elsbeth was up, probably working in her office. He turned from the door to glance out at the violent waves, thinking what a great day it would be for surfers. When he turned back, he caught a glimpse of his mother, stepping back from the window beside the door.

"Elsbeth, open the door," Adragon yelled and pounded harder when she continued to ignore him. Then he moved over to rattle the huge plate glass window with his fists. He stopped when he heard the bolt slide on the other side of the door.

Elsbeth had circles under her eyes but they only served to make her look aesthetic and more attractive than ever. She was wearing tight leggings and an oversized sweater in a flattering shade of blue. Her hair was curly and shower-damp, her face scrubbed as clean as a child's. The house would be too warm, but that was better than the cold, pounding wind off the ocean Adragon was leaving outside.

"If you've come for the rest of your things, I haven't had time to pack them yet," she said without looking at him.

"May I come in?" He stepped around her without waiting for an answer, and she sighed as she closed the door behind him.

"I don't have time to chat with you, Adragon, I'm working on chapter seven, and it's turned out to be difficult, so—"

She let the thought hang, and he felt a sudden surge of anger.

"Fuck chapter seven, Mother, I need to talk to you."

"Watch your language in my house, young man."

"I know it's your house, Elsbeth, you don't have to rub it in."

"Do you want something specific, Adragon, or did you come here to pick a fight with me?"

"I want to talk to you," he enunciated clearly, putting his face close to hers, forcing her to acknowledge him with her eyes, which were as cloudy as the sky over the sea.

"You look wonderful," he said, before he realized that he was going to say it. She did, warm and cold, dark and light, the most interesting woman he had ever known.

"Save it, Adragon. I told you I'm busy."

"Okay," he said without further preamble, "tell me about my father."

Silence, then a burst of unflattering laughter. "Tell you what? Tell you how he walked out on us? Don't tell me you want to find the bastard and explore your roots or something?"

"I have to know about him, it's important."

"Why?" she asked, suspicion narrowing her eyes to slits.

"Mother, I'm seventeen years old and I haven't seen my father for at least fifteen years. I don't remember what he looked like, I don't know anything about him. I don't remember ever seeing a picture of him. Now something's come up and I have to know, and you're the only one who can tell me."

Elsbeth seemed to be considering her son's request for several long minutes before she answered. "He's dead," she said, and Adragon felt the room tilt under his feet. She ran to him and let him lean on her tiny frame until the room righted itself and he could stand alone. Then he followed her to the airy, plant-filled kitchen where she put coffee in the percolator, added water, and plugged it in.

"I have a picture of him in my office, in the bottom of the drawer where I keep my private papers. He was a good-looking man, a charmer, totally irresponsible. You're nothing like him, thank God!"

Adragon sat on a kitchen chair while she busied herself laying out croissants with a butter substitute and sugar-free jam.

"I don't want to eat," he protested when she set a plate in front of him, but she pushed it an inch closer and he realized that he was hungry, in spite of just hearing that his father was dead.

"Don't think you have to mourn, Adragon. He never meant anything to you when he was alive."

"You're so damned practical, aren't you? He must have meant something to you once."

"Once, a long, long time ago. I can hardly remember why. I suppose it was the sex. You're learning how that can be, aren't you?"

121

He wanted to hurt her, and she was surely asking for it. "What Del and I have is unimaginable, Elsbeth."

"Spare me the details." She sloshed coffee from the cup she placed in front of him, but missed spilling it in his lap, which was probably her intention.

As they drank their coffee, Elsbeth filled Adragon in on the small, unimportant details of his father's life. While he was married to Elsbeth, the man had been an X-ray technician in a large New Jersey hospital. After their divorce, which had been initiated by Elsbeth, he had literally disappeared from the face of the earth. He had never paid child support, and never asked for visitation rights, even though Adragon was his only child. When he died from pneumonia, some well-meaning person had sent Elsbeth a clipping from the obituary column.

They took their refills to the living room, where Adragon sat on the couch beneath the window that framed the ocean and waited for Elsbeth to dig out the picture of his father. When she put it on the table in front of him, he wished that he hadn't insisted on seeing it. Finally, he lifted the photograph and gazed into the eyes of a man of indeterminate age, with a rather nondescript appearance. Brown hair several shades lighter than his son's, blue eyes, fair complexion. One of a million men who might have fathered a child and walked away, but not the man who fathered a vampire child. Adragon knew.

In the photograph, the man's gaze was fixed on a baby nestled in the arms of a young, vibrant Elsbeth. She looked exactly as Adragon looked today. No, that wasn't true. She looked exactly as he had looked several weeks ago, before the vampire thing started.

"He was a handsome, charming man, but he was no damned good."

"The way he's looking at the child, at me—"

She flew across the room and grabbed the photograph out of Adragon's hands, crumpled it, and tossed it to the floor.

"He looked at me that way, too. Believe me, it didn't mean a damned thing."

"What happened? You've never told me why he left you."

"When he got tired of us, he left, that's all there was to it."

"I don't believe you."

She looked surprised for a split second, then smiled as she shrugged her thin shoulders. "So, don't believe me."

Adragon carried the empty coffee cups to the kitchen. When he returned to the living room, his mother was standing in front of the big picture window, staring off into the distance. He had never seen her look so vulnerable. He saw for a moment the Elsbeth of the photograph, young and in love, the woman who had suffered the betrayal of her beloved. The mood lasted only a moment before his mother was back with him, her dark blue eyes flashing with anger.

"I've always been sorry the bastard didn't live long enough to see how well we did without him."

Adragon left her there without saying goodbye, and went home to Del, who seemed to sense that something important had happened to him, something that he wasn't ready to share with her. She left him alone that night, and called him from work the next day to tell him that three donors would be coming to the condo that evening.

"Oh," he said finally, "is it that time of the month again?" She obviously didn't think his remark was worthy of a reply. "Why three?" he asked finally, admitting

123

to himself that despite his increased physical strength Del still had the upper hand in their relationship.

"I've asked Weldon to join us this evening. I knew you wouldn't mind."

"Who the hell is Weldon?" he asked, spitting out the word as if it left a bad taste in his mouth.

"You met him the night you attended the Society meeting with your mother. He's about your age, with blond, curly hair?"

"Vaguely." He did remember: the boy who had answered the door to them and fawned all over Elsbeth.

"Well, you can meet him again tonight if you want to. Otherwise, just stay out of his way."

Adragon was in a bad mood all day. He felt a strange excitement when he thought of the donors, and that made him even more angry. When they finally arrived, accompanied by Del and a smiling Weldon, Adragon insisted on choosing first. The girl he chose was tiny and pale with stringy hair and huge brown eyes. She looked as if she had been ill for a long time, and Adragon almost hoped that she had a contagious disease, although he knew that wasn't very likely, since the Society of Vampires was very strict about the donors' required physicals.

He took Lolita (she actually told him her name with a straight face) to the master bedroom before Del could raise an objection, and told her to strip for him. It was obvious that she wasn't used to removing her clothing before an audience, but she tried, and it was her innocent quality that finally turned Adragon on.

When the girl was naked, Adragon took a razor blade out of his shaving kit and showed it to her. Her complexion turned a shade whiter, but she didn't flinch. He held out his hand, and she trustingly extended her own, palm upward, exposing the purple veins of her wrist. Adragon lifted her hand and traced the veins under her milky skin with his fingertip. She shivered and closed her eyes, in either fear or anticipation, Adragon couldn't tell which.

He undressed himself quickly and sat down on the edge of the bed, then pulled the small girl between his knees. He held her narrow thighs in the vice of his powerful knees, and sliced into the veins of her wrist. She sighed, but didn't scream out, as he had feared she might. Her eyes rolled back into her head, and she slumped forward.

Adragon fell on top of her and slurped the blood from the fountain that sprayed out across the pristine white sheets of Del's bed. Then he lifted the girl's arm and clamped his mouth to the ruptured vein, finding the touch of her human flesh on his lips while he fed far more satisfying. He sucked noisily, as the hot liquid filled his mouth and flooded down his throat. His veins felt as if they would burst, and his heartbeat accelerated until it was pumping at at least twice its normal rate.

He was filled, but not satisfied. The fact that the girl's blood was not as sweet as Del's made him want to hurt her, to rip her arm to gory pieces and waste her offending blood. He tore at the wound with his teeth and sucked harder, intent on punishing her. He didn't hear the bedroom door open, and wasn't aware that anyone had entered the room until he felt a strong arm lock across his throat and cut off his air supply. He shot his eyes to the left and saw Weldon's blond curls.

"Let me go, you son of a bitch," he screamed. "This isn't any of your business."

"You kill somebody in Del's apartment, it's my business," Weldon panted, as he pulled Adragon from the bed, freeing the girl, Lolita.

Adragon hit the floor hard, and either Weldon or Del

125

must have struck him over the head with something because when he came to apparently just minutes later, Del was bending over Lolita, using her lips to close the wounds in the girl's arm.

"You have the nerve to call someone else a son of a bitch?" Del asked calmly when she turned her attention away from her patient. "You just can't handle this, can you, Adragon?"

"Where did you hide him?"

"I told him to go."

"Was he afraid of me?"

"He has been a vampire since the age of seven, Adragon. He could have hurt you badly if he'd wanted to."

"I'll bet." Adragon sat up and leaned against the wall, watching the girl start to come around. "What do you do with the bad vampires, Del? What will you do with me, put a stake through my heart and bury me alive in unhallowed ground?"

"You're not funny."

"No, I'm not. And I'm not a vampire either."

"What are you then?" she asked with a sadness in her voice that touched Adragon and made him hate her.

"I'm a hybrid, half-human, half-vampire, a being who can't live in either world now, a misfit."

"No." She shook her head back and forth, and her long red hair sent sparks flying across the room.

"Yes, that's what I am, Del, you'll see. I'll never be a proper vampire. Never."

Del didn't smile, and she didn't come to him that night when he lay in the little guest room, his veins filled to capacity with blood that was far too bitter to satisfy his needs.

He didn't answer the telephone when it rang the next day, and he didn't turn on any lights in the apartment although the day was dark and gloomy. He stood before the mirror where such a short time ago he had admired his newfound strength and confidence, and stared at the stranger he had become. Even as he tried to deny it, desire coursed through his veins and spread through his body. Desire for blood, a wild, raging desire to fill his veins with the rich, sweet fluid that sustained him. He knew that this would be the course his life would take from this day forward: desire, fulfillment, then disgust at his act, and dissatisfaction when the blood was not rich enough or sweet enough.

He needed a victim, he needed someone to hurt, he needed Del, and she walked through the door at precisely the wrong moment.

"I thought vampires had a sixth sense or something," he said by way of greeting.

She nodded, mumbled "sometimes," and sat down the deli bag of goodies that were to serve as dinner.

"Then why didn't you sense that you should have stayed away tonight?"

He was naked to the waist, his body glistening with sweat, his breath ragged.

"I knew. But you're my responsibility, aren't you?"

"Am I, Del? Am I your responsibility? Or am I Elsbeth's responsibility? My father is dead, did you know that? Of course, you knew that."

She anticipated his movements but she wasn't fast enough to get away from him. He leapt across the room with lightning speed and slammed into her, scattering cheese and olives and roast beef across the counter and onto the floor. He pinned her to the wall and bit her neck savagely, ripping away chunks of tender flesh. Blood darkened her white silk blouse and he wallowed in it, sucking it through his nose, breathing it in.

"My life," he murmured, tossing his head, throwing

crimson droplets across the room, "you give me life."

"You'll kill me," she said weakly, but she may as well have taken her punishment silently because Adragon didn't hear her pleas for mercy. He drank from her ruined throat until he was sated, then sank down beside her on the floor and licked the wound in her neck until the bleeding stopped. He left her there, alone in the eerily quiet condo.

He would never remember how he got to the house. He appeared to jump to the deck, barely touching the steps, hardly feeling the impact when he slammed into the heavy back door. He had to butt the door twice before it gave, sending splinters of wood and shards of glass flying into the kitchen. He stood in the middle of the room and bellowed his mother's name until she appeared in the doorway, a black-clad apparition.

"How dramatic," she drawled, taking in the scattered slivers of wood that had been her door and her son's wild appearance. "Am I supposed to be frightened?"

He crossed the room in two strides and clamped his powerful hands on her shoulders. She was thin and white, trembling in spite of her show of bravado, and it gave him pleasure to know that he was leaving bruises on her pale skin under her black jumpsuit. He knew that he could hurt her badly, even kill her, if he chose to do so. She started to struggle, and he shook her roughly back and forth, watching the way her head wobbled on her spindly neck. When she stopped struggling, he picked her up easily and carried her into her bedroom. From the doorway, he tossed her across the room, not gently. She landed on the bed, bounced once, and slid over the side of the mattress onto the floor. That was where he left her, the second woman he had abandoned within an hour.

Adragon didn't return home that night; he slept in a

128

flophouse in Asbury Park for three nights before he got up the nerve to check and see if Del was still alive. Could a vampire kill another vampire the way he had attacked Del? He wasn't sure and he didn't want to find out the hard way. She answered the telephone when he finally got the courage to dial, and his sense of relief almost overwhelmed him. He held himself up by his elbows, which rested on the little metal shelf in the phone booth, and let his legs dangle uselessly beneath him. When he left the booth, his legs still trembled but he felt better than he had in days.

He drove up the shore with the Mustang's top down, intensely aware of the frigid air and the biting wind, the smell of salt off the sea and the power of the fast car which he controlled.

"I have the power!" he shouted into the wind as it rushed past him, and his words reverberated through his head and rocked his body, even as he swiped at his eyes to wipe away the tears of relief.

A block short of Elsbeth's house, Adragon cut the engine; closer to the house, he killed the lights. He let the car coast to a stop under the pilings, and soundlessly opened the door. He stood beneath the house for several minutes, hidden in its huge shadow, listening carefully for any sounds from above. His hearing was so keen that he thought he could hear sea birds taking tiny footsteps in the sand several hundred feet away. It took only seconds for him to make the decision that Elsbeth was not in the house. He heard the hum of the refrigerator, the faint movement of the hands on the grandfather clock in the hallway and several other insignificant sounds that he had never before consciously separated from the sound of his own breath or the sound of the sea crashing behind him.

Adragon waited several minutes more, then climbed

the steps and crossed the deck to the restored kitchen door. When he'd thrown his keys at Elsbeth the night he left home, he hadn't bothered to tell her that he had a second key to the kitchen door in a secret compartment in his wallet. Now he pulled out the small metal object and inserted it in the lock, half-expecting it to stick and refuse to turn. It didn't. The lock clicked and the door swung open when he turned the knob.

There was a low-watt bulb burning over the range, and it gave the room a homey look that hit Adragon in the pit of his stomach. He almost expected to see the Cleavers enter from stage right. He was overcome with the desire to live here again, to share meals with his mother, to sit under the windows in her office and watch her work, to let her check his blood sugar and scold him when he didn't keep his diet. Then he remembered the reason behind his homecoming and the moment passed.

In his mother's bathroom, he peed in the marble sink and stared at his reflection in the mirror. A stranger stared back at him: a man with a three-day growth of beard, straggly hair, and wild, red-rimmed eyes. He smiled when he thought about how he would scare Elsbeth. "Wicked, really wicked," he said aloud, and his smile broadened.

He splashed cold water on his face, dried it with the expensive, hand-embroidered towel he had never been allowed to use when he lived there, and began to systematically search his mother's house.

Chapter Fourteen

Adragon started in the kitchen, since that was the least likely place he would be expected to be prowling around and accidentally happen on anything Elsbeth was trying to hide from him. He opened the left-hand wall cabinet over the counter and examined the contents thoroughly. Cups and saucers, cereal bowls in Elsbeth's everyday Corning Ware pattern. He checked out the middle cabinet which was practically empty, and moved on to the one on the right-hand side. It contained the staples of Elsbeth's gourmet (a definite joke) kitchen: sugar, flour, several different salt substitutes, including sea salt and Mrs. Dash, and about a hundred boxes of sugar-free jello and pudding mix. He shook each of the boxes, then placed it back on the shelf in exactly the same position. Not much to sift through in the refrigerator either. So much for the kitchen.

He made a desultory check of the living room, dining room, and his own vacated quarters. The way the house was designed and built, none of the rooms had many nooks or crannies. The design was sparse, clean, long expanses of white walls uncluttered with art work or knickknacks. To Elsbeth's way of thinking, anything that wasn't absolutely necessary was excess. She didn't try to adorn her house with ornaments, to make it appear more interesting to other people. The house was for her own enjoyment and (once) Adragon's. So, he wasn't surprised when he found nothing in any of the rooms he examined, nothing that he hadn't seen before, nothing that didn't belong there.

He hesitated only a moment before he opened the door to Elsbeth's bedroom. Old habits die hard, and this room had been available to him by invitation only from the first day they moved into the house. "You are old enough to understand," Elsbeth had told him in her "mommy" voice, "that I will require my privacy. When you need something, you will knock on the door and wait for me to answer. You must *never* enter my room without knocking."

Her words had hurt Adragon a little at first. They had shared everything, even a bedroom for a while when he was eight or nine, when there wasn't enough money for a two-bedroom apartment. But he found it easy enough to live with her terms, since he had the rest of the big, beautiful house to himself. He was suddenly flooded with memories of how proud he had once been to live in this house, and of how he had bragged to his friends that he and his mother were moving to the exclusive shore community.

Once inside, he walked to the middle of the room and twirled around slowly, his eyes keenly examining the surface of the fruitwood dresser, the chest, the matching nightstands. Elsbeth's private sanctuary, like the rest of the house, was sparsely furnished in a traditional style that was entirely her own. She longed to be comfortable in the first home she had ever owned, and didn't much care whether she impressed her few, carefully chosen guests.

There was little to search; the woman of the house had several expensive outfits hung in a deep built-in wardrobe. The rest of her clothing consisted of jeans and T-shirts, leggings and sweaters, clothing designed for someone half her age but worn well by the stick-thin Elsbeth.

Adragon's hands started to sweat as he rifled through her underwear drawer and leaned over the bed where she slept to feel around beneath the mattress.

"What in the hell am I looking for?" he asked himself aloud when after several minutes in the room he came up empty. "Proof, I'm looking for proof," he answered himself. "And what would that be?" he asked. A none-too-elegant shrug was the answer to that one.

"Damn it to hell!" In frustration, he swung around and exited the bedroom, not yet ready to give up on his search. Several minutes later, in a jimmied drawer in Elsbeth's office, he got the first hint that it might not be in vain. Adragon recognized the architect's plans for the house the moment he saw the roll of blue-tinted drawings. When the building was in progress, Elsbeth had carried a set of them around with her, as if she had to be in control of every phase of the operation. Now Adragon wanted to know why. He spread the oversize sheets of paper out on his mother's desk and leaned over them, moving his hand from one room to the next, squinting to read the tiny print that explained (probably for Elsbeth's benefit) exactly what each square or squiggle signified.

It was beautiful. There was nothing to decode, nothing to decipher. In tiny white print, Elsbeth's secret was spelled out for all the world to see: small private room to be located behind master bedroom, entrance to be gained through sliding touch-sensitive control panel located on north wall, two feet from juncture with east wall.

Adragon left the plans on the desk and raced back through his mother's bedroom, straight to the spot that had been marked on the plans. He tapped on the wall in several places until he heard a resounding echo that indicated a hollow spot. He struck the wall with his fist. It moved. He watched with fascination as a panel to the right of the dresser receded a few inches, then slid slowly to the left. Within seconds, there was a space large enough for him to enter.

He stepped through the opening and was hit by a blast of cold air: air conditioning in January. He was standing in a walk-in refrigerator, hidden behind a secret panel in his mother's bedroom. He let out a whoop and gave himself a high-five. This was what he'd been looking for; he'd hit pay dirt.

The room wasn't big by any standards, probably four by six feet. It contained a small metal table, a metal cabinet which held syringes, alcohol wipes and Band Aids, and several recessed shelves built into the wall. He reached out and touched one of the few items Elsbeth had left on the shelves, a tiny bottle filled with dark red liquid. Adragon's smile widened as he stared down at what he held in his hand: a vial of blood with his own name scrawled across the white pharmaceutical label.

There were two more vials on the shelves, and Adragon snatched them up and bounced all three off

134

the walls of the hidden room. He knew with certainty that he had discovered an enclave of evil in the midst of what he had been led to believe was a normal house inhabited by seemingly normal people. But he and Elsbeth were not normal; he knew that now. The word swelled in his brain until it exploded and he screamed it into the silence of the alien room. "VAMPIRE!"

He recovered the three vials of blood which had hit the walls and bounced soundlessly to the black and white tiled floor. He ran to the kitchen and threw them in the sink, where they once again refused to break. He had to hit them several times with the hammer Elsbeth kept in the kitchen drawer before they shattered and splashed the sink and the counter with crimson gore.

He stood leaning over the sink, breathing hard, his anger a living thing that threatened to take over and control him. He knew that in his present state he could not trust himself to encounter Elsbeth and act rationally. He found this knowledge stupefying, since in his seventeen years he had never raised his hand to his mother until the past week. As a matter of fact, he had never raised his hand to anyone, male or female, unless it was a matter of self-defense.

Adragon left the blood in the sink and took a cold shower in his old bathroom, which smelled of mildew in spite of the fact that it looked spotlessly clean. When he returned to the living room, he noticed that the sun had set and the sea outside the windows was dark. He had no idea what time he had arrived at the house or how long he had been there but it occurred to him that Elsbeth would probably be returning home soon. The cold water splashing on his body had cooled him, and he now felt calm enough to sit down and wait for her. He left the house dark, locked the kitchen door so that she wouldn't suspect an intruder, and hoped that his scent wouldn't give him away.

While he waited, he took several deep breaths and watched behind closed lids as visions from his childhood swam before him. He had been diagnosed as a juvenile diabetic when he was seven years old, but Elsbeth had never let him become depressed by his illness or by the prospect that there was no cure for diabetes. She was an LPN, working on assignment to housebound terminally ill patients in the Asbury Park area. She seemed to know all there was to know about life and death, and she knew that her son would live a long, long life. Adragon had felt that his mother had inside knowledge of the intricate workings of fate. If Elsbeth said there was nothing to fear from diabetes, then there was nothing to fear. End of discussion. His childhood had been secure. He had never felt deprived because of his medical condition.

Actually, he realized for the first time that his illness had been the reason for the strong bond he had forged with his mother. He had needed her, and she had used that need to hold him in check, to keep him by her side while other boys roamed the streets of Asbury Park looking for girls. He had never played team sports, never played a musical instrument, never had a birthday party. And he had never resented any of it until this moment.

Adragon's mind was so clear tonight, his thoughts stretched out, and he began to understand so many things. Up until the past month, his relationship with Elsbeth must have seemed unnatural to many

136

people. They not only looked alike, but they thought alike. They *were* alike, more alike than even he had realized. But everything had changed with the coming of Del Keelan into his life, and now he was hiding in the shadows, waiting to attack his mother.

He moved to stand in the hallway where he could watch the kitchen door without being observed, not that he needed to see her with his eyes. He smelled her scent and sensed her presence before he heard the Jag roar up the street and stop beneath the house, before he heard her small, sandaled foot touch the bottom step. She slid her hand up the banister and climbed slowly, both feet touching each step, as though she might be very tired, and Adragon felt himself begin to soften toward her. He quickly squelched the feeling and by the time the door opened at the turn of her key, he hated her almost as much as he loved her, and was glad that she obviously hadn't scanned the house for a foreign scent before entering.

In the heavy silence, it would have been easy for anyone to hear her quick intake of breath when she caught the odor of the blood in the sink with her keen sense of smell and then honed in on it with her perfect night vision. Her eyes searched for her son and found him, and Adragon saw everything that he was and everything she thought of him in her glance before either of them spoke. He only now remembered that he had hoped to scare her with his unkempt appearance, then ruined his own plan by taking a shower.

"I always thought if I came face to face with a vampire, I'd know it," he said. "You know: fangs, pasty white skin, nasty odor from sleeping in a box

137

of dirt in the cellar."

"How foolish of you," she answered, dismissing him.

He grabbed her arm and swung her around, forcing her to pay attention to his words.

"You know, up until now, I thought it was a game. I thought we were all playing some kind of foolish, dangerous game, like the drug experiments of the sixties. Something we could stop when we tired of it. I thought the donors were cool, acting as if they were feeding vampires, knowing it was make-believe. But you know what, Elsbeth? They were all laughing at me behind my back, the naive boy vampire, ignorant of his background, denying his true nature. Were you laughing, too, Elsbeth?"

He squeezed her arm and she grimaced. "You're hurting me, Adragon. Don't forget that I'm still your mother, no matter what you think of me."

"You want to know what I think of you, Mother? I think you're a real bitch."

She swung at him, aiming for his face, but he easily sidestepped the blow and laughed at her frustration.

"I'm not afraid of you anymore, Elsbeth, isn't that amazing? And I'll tell you why I'm not afraid of you."

"Don't bother."

"Oh, no bother. The reason I'm not afraid of you is because . . ." He took a step forward and shoved his face close to hers, knowing that she hated to have anyone invade her space. ". . . because I'm a vampire, Elsbeth. V-A-M-P-I-R-E, vampire with a capital 'V'."

The look of shock reflected on her face wasn't convincing. She already knew that he knew, just as he had suspected.

"Doesn't surprise you, huh?"

"You're crazy."

"Crazy like a fox, Mother dear."

"What do you want from me, Adragon?" This time he let her turn her face and walk away from him but he watched her back, the tension in her shoulders, the unnatural stillness of her constantly moving hands.

"Why did you do it?"

"Do what, Adragon? Is this going to be another one of your dreary guessing games?" God, she was good, he had to give her that. If he held a knife to her throat, she wouldn't just give in and get it over with without a battle.

"Why did you hide my true nature from me, Mother? Why did you let me have no knowledge of my vampirism, even though I suffered from a human disease that could have killed me while I was still a child?"

"Don't be so damned dramatic. You were never in any danger of dying." She seemed to glide across the floor until she was standing only inches from Adragon, staring into his eyes with her own dark eyes flashing sparks of cold fire. "I watched you every moment, I loved you as no mother should ever love a child. You were my entire world. So don't ever accuse me of putting you in danger."

Elsbeth turned on her heel and retreated from the kitchen. Once he overcame the shock of realizing that she wasn't going to deny that she was a vampire, Adragon caught up with her.

"But you could have let me be a vampire," he persisted, "and the diabetes would have gone away."

"That's not the way it works, all vampires are not immune to human disease. You were born human, the veil covered your eyes. There was nothing I could do to reverse that. You tell me that you think you're a vampire now, but you still have your diabetes."

"And I always will?" Adragon felt tired and defeated, sorry that he had forced this confrontation before he'd had more time to think things out.

"In this lifetime," Elsbeth answered tenderly, "you will always be a diabetic, and although I blame myself for that, I am incapable of changing that part of your life."

"I see." He didn't, but he would tuck that question away in the back of his mind for now. There was something more important he needed to know. "He left because he found out, didn't he?"

"Could you be a little more specific?"

"He, meaning my father, left us because he found out that you were a vampire, didn't he?"

"Yes." She turned to face Adragon and her smile was triumphant. "I bit him, I threatened to make him one of us. I offered to share eternity with him, and the poor, unimaginative fool ran for his life."

"You drove him away and then you hated him for leaving."

"Exactly." She tilted her chin and viewed her son with the same haughty, amused expression that she had probably given his father as he had backed away from her in fear and distaste.

Adragon edged past her and slid the dead bolt on the kitchen door, then attached the chain.

"What are you doing?" she asked, and by way of answer Adragon took her by the arm and led her down the hallway to a room at the back of the house, which had once been his favorite room, but now was seldom used. It was furnished with built-in book-shelves, a flowered couch, a few armchairs, and an oversize table scattered with magazines and old man-uscripts. Still holding Elsbeth's arm, Adragon slid two chairs closer together, then shoved her into one of them.

"What the hell do you think you're doing?" she asked again, not trying to hide the fact that she was getting more angry by the minute.

"We're going to talk, Mother," Adragon growled close to her face. "You and your vampire son are go-ing to get a few things straight between them."

"It's late and I'm tired. Can't this wait until tomor-row?"

"This can't wait until one minute later than it is right now, Elsbeth. Start talking."

"What?"

"I want you to tell me everything, from the date of my conception to the present, and I have to warn you that it won't make me happy if I find out you've lied to me."

"My God, what do you want from me?"

"The truth," he answered simply, forcing her ges-turing hands into her lap and holding them there. "Now tell me what I want to know, or I'll shake the shit out of you."

Adragon watched his mother's face change as she realized that this was one battle she wasn't going to win. She sat back in the chair, folded her hands in her lap, and stared off into space for several long, si-lent minutes. Adragon didn't rush her. He knew that in time she would tell him everything he wanted to know. The long black night stretched out in front of him, and he was content to spend it here in this room that occupied a fond place in his memory. His mind reached out to make contact with his mother's keen intellect. She looked into his eyes, he felt her consciousness meld with his, and he understood that there would be no words necessary for her to pass on to him all the knowledge she had withheld for seventeen years.

Chapter Fifteen

Hours later, Adragon and his mother sat on opposite sides of the table, their hands joined, their eyes locked. Elsbeth's eyes sparkled as she reclaimed her son with her words. Adragon knew that she was not sad that he had learned the wonderful/awful secret of his vampirism. She was obviously relieved that she would no longer have to lie to him about either his past or his future. He leaned forward and listened intently as she continued in her deep, velvety voice.

"We have lived for hundreds of years, Adragon, for many more years than you can imagine now. But soon"—Elsbeth squeezed his hand and favored him with a smile—"soon you will feel the limitations of your humanity begin to give way to an omniscient knowledge. At the time of your birth, I deprived you of this knowledge by drawing the veil over your eyes, and I've hated Del Keelan for trying to pierce that veil. But now—now you and I will part the veil."

"Go on," he urged, returning the pressure on her hand, "tell me everything."

"Hundreds of years . . . we have been friend and lover, sister and brother, husband and wife. Always together, we have been joined by loyalty and lust, by blood, by miracles of birth and death. We have been separated for periods of time by the savagery of mortal man and the vagaries of time, but never for long and never by our own decision. Never. It is our fate to be together always, and our destiny. You believe that now, don't you, Adragon?"

"Yes," he vowed with a passion he had never felt before, at least, not in this lifetime, "you are my destiny." But the avowal was not a complete surrender to his mother's will. A part of him wanted to run, to pull his hand away from Elsbeth's and get the hell out of that house before it was too late. He felt as if she had buried her hooks in him again, and was getting ready to reel him in, to put him in a box and deprive him of the rest of his life. He laughed aloud then, remembering that life would go on forever in one form or another, now that he was a vampire.

He closed his eyes and Del's gorgeous face swam into view, her long strawberry hair, her wild green eyes. He would never let Elsbeth keep him away from Del.

At the same time, another part of him swelled with pride at being Elsbeth's son, the son who had been her lover in another life. That's what she had called him: her lover. That son, that other-life lover adored the woman who sat across from him, gazing at him with maternal pride.

"Adragon . . ."

"Yes, Mother."

"I want to show you all the things we've shared, the bodies we've inhabited."

"Show me?"

"Yes." She gave him no further explanation, and he asked none.

"Okay," he said finally, "but—"

When he hesitated, Elsbeth squeezed his hand again. "You can ask me anything, darling, anything at all."

"Have we always been vampires, or were we once normal human beings?"

Anger flashed in her eyes but she quickly overcame it. "We are 'normal' now, Adragon. Once we were only ordinary humans, but that was so long ago that I can barely remember what it was like."

"I still don't understand why you know all about it and I don't. Why did I forget? Why didn't you tell me?"

"The veil, darling, remember?"

He shook his head impatiently and let go of her hand, to break the contact so that he could think clearly. "You covered my eyes with the veil, all right, but what does that mean? And why did you do it, were you angry with me, had you finally tired of me?"

"I will explain everything to you in time, Adragon. You must trust me, and let me move at my own pace."

"One more question: Were you ever going to tell me? If Del hadn't taught me about my true nature, would I have gone through my entire life without knowing?"

"That's a question I can't answer, Adragon." Her eyes had clouded over as quickly as storm clouds cross the sun. "I always wanted to tell you but as time went on, it became more and more difficult."

"But why, Mother, I have to know why you did it."

"No," she snapped, "no more. We will do this my way or not at all. If you choose to leave now . . ." She waved her hand in a sweeping gesture, and Adragon considered rising from his chair and moving toward

145

the door, calling her bluff. But in the end, he bowed his head, and acknowledged her superiority. She could control him now, but it wouldn't last long. Adragon knew that as he gained knowledge, he would grow stronger, and he suddenly realized that Elsbeth knew it, too. There were many more questions he wanted to ask, but he grasped his mother's hands, stared into the mirrors of her eyes, and kept his silence.

Elsbeth, too, remained silent but her thoughts penetrated Adragon's subconscious mind and lulled him into a deep sleep. He dreamed, and the world opened up before him, wide vistas he had only imagined were his to explore. He was young and old, male and female, peasant and intellectual. He was everything, everywhere, stretching out to the limits of the earth, and Elsbeth was always by his side. They wore the finest garments, and ate sumptuous feasts. They hid in caves, naked and hungry. Dogs hunted them down as if they were animals, and monarchs sought their favor. They were good and evil, but never completely one or the other, because the good in one always balanced out the evil in the other, and Adragon understood that they shared one soul between them and that it would always be so.

He saw himself in filthy rags, with long blood-encrusted incisors, running down a sloping path. He cast his glance to the side and saw that his partner was a carbon copy of himself, not clearly male nor female. Then his rags changed to a velvet suit with fine lace dripping at the cuff. The woman whose tiny hand rested on his arm was exquisite, one of the most beautiful women he had ever seen. They were dancing in a magnificent ballroom, and they were very much in love.

146

The next picture was one of a swimming pool, large and luxurious by Jersey Shore standards. Adragon zeroed in on two people lying close to each other on oversize striped beach towels. Both bodies were bronze and perfectly shaped; both heads were covered with platinum hair; both sets of eyes were pale blue. They were identical twins, and when they moved toward each other, Adragon could not tell which body was his. Elsbeth's voice boomed in his head like the voice of God, "We were driven to sin because something went wrong that wasn't our fault. We chose to be lovers and were reincarnated as twins."

Adragon suddenly remembered, and he felt the same hot desire he had felt for his sister that awful day in California when he —

The memory faded and Elsbeth sat across from him, smiling a secretive little smile. "That's enough for today," she told him. She was obviously waiting for an argument, but Adragon was speechless for several minutes.

"Is there more like that?" he asked finally, not sure what his reaction should be.

"I told you that was a mistake. It wasn't our fault."

"Does that mean that God — wait, don't interrupt me. Does that mean that some guiding force in the universe put a barrier between us? Does it mean that someone or something tried to stop us?"

"Don't let your imagination run away with you, darling. You've been through a lot in the past hours, now I think you should retire to your room and rest. Sleep, if you can, and I'll wake you for dinner."

"But Del will be expecting me to come home," he protested halfheartedly.

"This is your home," Elsbeth answered sweetly,

"here with me. This is where you belong."

And she was right. It was.

He had walked through time and he had seen the whole earth in what seemed like minutes, but Adragon wasn't tired or thirsty or hungry. He could still taste on his tongue the coffee Elsbeth had brewed for him before they started to talk.

Elsbeth released his hands, and Adragon felt a jolt, as if he had just let go of a live electrical wire. He left the table and walked over to the window that looked out to the sea. He pulled the heavy fabric drapes aside and was momentarily blinded by the bright sunlight that reflected off the water. He realized that he had no idea what day it was, or how many sunrises he had spent in this room with his mother, but he knew it was more than one because no one could change as much as he had changed in the short space of a few hours.

The sight of the sun rising above the water was the most beautiful thing he had ever seen. How many mornings had he walked on the beach and watched the sun come up? Thousands, probably. But it was different today because he saw it now through the eyes of a person who had roamed the earth for hundreds of years and survived on the blood of animals and children, gypsies and kings. The seventeen-year-old Adragon found himself both admiring and loathing that person.

"Are you hungry?" his mother asked from somewhere behind him. "Should I fix you some breakfast before you lie down?"

"Yes, I think I'm hungry," he answered without turning around. He wasn't really hungry, but eating would give him something to do, an excuse to stop

148

thinking and put off the next decision he would have to make.

"Why do we eat and drink?" he asked, as he watched Elsbeth assemble an omelet. "In all the novels I've read, the vampires subsist on blood alone."

"There are a lot of superstitions," Elsbeth answered, "surely Del told you that."

"Do you mind the questions now?"

"I love your questions, Adragon, so long as they don't get too serious. I love having you home, feeding you, looking at you." She left her task just long enough to plant a kiss on his forehead and push a lock of his dark hair off his face.

"Mom, this question is really weird."

"Go on."

"Can you remember . . . the other lives? No, that's not what I mean. Do you remember them all the time? Like now, do you just see me as your son, the way we are now, or do the other lives kind of overlap this one sometimes?"

"Of course not," she answered, as she spooned eggs onto his plate. Then she raised her eyes to meet his and finished answering. "Not unless I let them."

Elsbeth poured two cups of coffee and sat down at the table to watch Adragon eat his eggs and toast. He ate as if he were hungry, in an attempt to hide the fact that her answer had upset him.

"You know," she mused, "I'm glad you had your little fling with Del."

He made a quick decision not to remark that it was more than "a little fling." Elsbeth would only believe what she wanted to believe anyway.

"Know why?" she asked him.

He shook his head and shoved another forkful of

149

the runny egg mixture into his mouth.

"Don't get mad at me now but — well, sometimes I wondered if you were gay."

Adragon spit the eggs onto his plate and shoved it away from him, what little appetite he had gone completely.

"Are you serious?" he asked.

She was smiling, and he wanted to wipe the stupid grin off her face. He felt his stomach rumbling, the eggs feeling like lead weights falling through his delicate intestines.

"Well, you didn't show much interest in girls, did you?"

"You *are* serious." He shook his head savagely back and forth and tried to dispel the anger rising in his chest. "Your memory doesn't serve you too well, Mother. Every time I got a date, I couldn't go because you needed me for something. You always had an excuse to keep me home, or drag me out to one of your speaking engagements as your escort."

"I enjoyed your company," Elsbeth answered defensively, "is it a crime to enjoy your son's company over that of a paid escort?"

"You never had to pay for anything like that in your life. There have always been lines of men, as far back as I can remember, men smelling around like you were a bitch in heat."

Before he realized what she was doing, she tossed the remains of her coffee in his face. The shock of the hot liquid hitting his skin propelled him into action. He stood too quickly, toppling his chair, brushing the china plate of cold eggs to the floor.

"You sick little bastard," Elsbeth screamed at him, anger painting her cheeks bright red. Her eyes blazed with fury and she looked around for a weapon, finally spotting a heavy wooden spoon that hung on a peg above the counter. She grabbed it and dove across the room, the spoon raised over her head. It struck him on the temple but he hardly felt the blow. He turned to face her and braced himself for another charge, but it never came. Instead, he was assaulted by a sharp bray of laughter.

It took him a moment to realize that Elsbeth was pointing at his face with the spoon, bent nearly double with helpless laughter. Watching her face contort, Adragon's shock quickly turned to amusement, then to hysteria. He reached out for his mother, and she fell into his arms. They leaned against each other and together they sank to the kitchen floor, slipping and sliding on the congealed remains of Adragon's breakfast. Elsbeth cried out when she landed on the handle of the spoon, which had so recently been her weapon, and Adragon laughed even harder. When their guffaws eased off, they were both out of breath, with tears streaming down their cheeks.

"You're a piece of work, Elsbeth," he told the woman who sat only inches away from him on the floor. He looked into her eyes, as he gently rolled a strand of her damp curly hair around his finger. Then the telephone rang shrilly, breaking into their moment, bringing them back to the real world and the year 1992, where Elsbeth was a nearly middle-aged woman and Adragon was her teenage son.

Elsbeth quickly rose to her feet and snatched up the telephone. "Hello," she said into the receiver, then "Yes," then "I'll call you back in five minutes."

"Business to tend to, darling," she told Adragon, and kissed him on the cheek in a very motherly way.

151

She retired to her bedroom to shower and change clothes and, Adragon assumed, to return the phone call she hadn't wanted him to listen to. Adragon held his breath, sure that she would come storming back out of her quarters, furious because he had broken into her secret room and caused so much damage. But minutes passed and there was no sound, except for the water running in the shower and the opening and closing of closet doors.

When even these small noises ceased, Adragon knew that Elsbeth was on the telephone, taking care of her "business." He wandered through the house, stopping in the living room to pick up his down jacket from the couch where he had tossed it the night he had come here to confront Elsbeth. The folded newspaper section he had taken from her desk drawer was still in his pocket. He shook it out flat on the coffee table and leaned over it. It was a copy of Section B of the *Asbury Park Press,* dated several weeks after he had left home to move in with Del. He thumbed through it twice before the right article caught his eye:

Asbury Park, N.J. Police here were called out yesterday to investigate a grisly find. Dozens of used hypodermic needles and vials containing what appeared to be blood washed up on the beach in an area just south of here. Detectives speculate that this could be waste from a hospital located north of the site where the trash was found, but hospital sources deny the accusation. Police from several surrounding municipalities are forming a task force to investigate.

Adragon ripped the article from the paper, folded it

quickly, and shoved it into his pocket. He crumpled the rest of the paper and took it out to the back porch, where he stuffed it down beneath the green plastic bag that contained Elsbeth's odorless garbage.

He was back in the kitchen, pouring cold water from a glass container into a gold-rimmed glass when Elsbeth reappeared. Her hair was still damp, her face shiny, and Adragon imagined for just a moment that she was his age, his twin, his soul mate.

"You look like a little kid," he told her, "are you sure you're my mother?"

"Flatterer. Now! What shall we do today? Should I call for lunch reservations? Or should we have a picnic on the porch with hot cocoa and blankets? Or a party? Yes, oh yes, that's what we'll do, we'll plan a party. What would you—"

She stopped abruptly and her sparkling eyes clouded over. Adragon had thrust his arms into his jacket. Now he was zipping it, turning the collar up to protect his neck from the cold.

"Oh, Adragon . . . no."

"Don't look at me that way, Mother. I didn't promise you anything."

"You belong here with me, in this house that we built together. We share the same soul, Adragon, I can't stand to be apart from you."

When Adragon said nothing, she turned on her heel and walked out of the room so fast that he had no time to form the words he should have said. He heard the door to her office slam, and he knew that there would be no talking to her now, not today. He opened the door and left his mother's house, cursing as he took the wooden steps two at a time and slid in the sand at the bottom.

153

He lost his balance for just a moment and was almost overcome by vertigo. He backed up and sat down hard on the bottom step, rested his swirling head in his hands, and massaged his aching temples. The fresh sea air and the short distance he had put between Elsbeth and himself had apparently caused some sort of a chemical reaction in his brain. Suddenly, he was overwhelmed by the fact that his mother had actually admitted to being a vampire. He felt as if he had just been hit over the head with a baseball bat. His head spun. It felt as if it might crack open at any second and spill his brains out onto the sand. His mind was running on overload, and he couldn't focus on any one clear thought for more than a second.

Vampire! An impossible word, a word that brought forth nothing but ridicule from today's society. Elsbeth was living out her worst horror story. Was it possible that this was why she wrote horror, rather than say, romance?

His father! Sometime when his head was clear, Adragon knew that he would have to think about his father, but not now, not while he felt this way. He wondered how he had been able to get away from her. She was so strong! Maybe she had wanted him to go for some reason. No, that wasn't the case. Then how? Maybe it was Del's doing, maybe Del was calling out to him, drawing him home. He only knew that once he had seen that newspaper clipping about the needles and the blood, he had to get out.

Just because the police had found needles washed up on the beach, that didn't necessarily mean that Elsbeth was responsible, did it? Didn't it? Elsbeth and how many others? The Society of Vampires?

Adragon's head continued to spin, but he pulled

himself to his feet and stumbled under the pilings of the house to his car.

He looked in the rearview mirror and confronted his own image: light growth of beard, crazy blue eyes, tousled dark hair.

"A vampire! Jesus Christ, man, I really am a vampire!"

Chapter Sixteen

Adragon stripped off his jacket, opened the driver's side door of the Mustang, and tossed the jacket in the backseat. He felt that he was being watched, and turned to find Raymond Sadler standing several hundred feet away, midway between his house and Elsbeth's.

Adragon ignored the older man and started to climb into the car.

"Adragon, wait, I want to speak to you," Raymond yelled over the noisy surf.

"Some other time, Ray," Adragon shouted back.

"I said I want to talk to you, boy."

"Fuck off, old man."

Adragon slammed the car door and pushed the button to lower the convertible top. He placed his hand on the gearshift knob, looked out the windshield, and nearly jumped off his seat. Raymond was standing directly in front of the car, his hands on the hood, his eyes boring into Adragon's.

"What the hell do you want?" Adragon asked but he didn't hear the man's answer. He was busy wondering how the hell Raymond had made it across the sand so fast. It was only seconds ago that he was standing halfway between the two houses, and the sand was the consistency of wet cement. A wave of cold fear washed over Adragon as he realized that he must have blacked out for several minutes, between the time he shouted at Raymond and the time he saw the man leaning on the hood of his car.

Raymond moved around to lean on the driver's side door, his face only inches from the boy's face.

"Where are you going?" he asked, as if it was any of his business.

"Home," Adragon replied, pumping the accelerator to make the Mustang's engine race.

"You are home, my boy. Surely, you're not planning to leave your mother again, because if you are—"

"If I am, what? Are you going to try and stop me?" Adragon laughed loudly, stomped the accelerator again, and Raymond stepped back from the car.

"You belong here with Elsbeth," Raymond stated simply.

"Is that your final argument?" Adragon couldn't stop laughing. Raymond looked so pitiful, so ineffectual. There was a high, cold wind off the ocean, and the man's sparse grayish-brown hair was being whipped around in all directions.

Raymond said something else then, something that Adragon couldn't quite make out, but it sounded like, "You will be held accountable," and that made Adragon laugh even harder.

"See you around, Ray," he mumbled, as he put the car in gear and stepped on the accelerator. The Mustang shot out from under the house, missed the paved driveway, slid in the wet sand and careened out onto the street, narrowly missing a brown station wagon full of kids. The driver turned to mouth an obscenity, and Adragon gave him the finger, which seemed to annoy the driver but amuse her small passengers.

Once he was on the main highway, Adragon passed the wagon and several other cars, until he was alone on the road, with nothing in front of him. He flipped on the state of the art radio just long enough to hear that it was twenty-six degrees on the Jersey Shore, with the threat of snow flurries.

"Alright," he said to the weatherman on the local station, "snow would be beautiful. The vampire boy loves snow."

Snow would cool him down, wouldn't it? Snow would cool down his blood, maybe make him feel as if he was normal again. Because right now, his blood was pounding hot in his veins, flooding into the chambers of his heart, throbbing in his temples. He felt the heat rising in his body, a blood high, a blood rush brought on by the realization and acknowledgment of his state. He had told himself before that he was a vampire, but now it was a certainty. Elsbeth was a vampire, and so was her little boy. He instinctively knew that this high wasn't a good thing, and that when he crashed, he would have to have blood, the way an addict would have to have drugs in a similar situation.

He was hot, and his clothes felt too small, too tight, too constricting. He unbuttoned his navy and green flannel shirt and slid his arms out of the sleeves, then tugged at his navy turtleneck until it covered his face and obscured his vision of the windy coastal road. One more tug and he could see again, just in time to avoid a collision with a black Mercedes and its very frightened driver. Adragon waved his turtleneck shirt at the man, then let go of it and watched it waft away on the breeze.

He tapped the brake pedal and slowed down, fighting off the desire to run naked across the sand and fling himself headfirst into the icy sea. He felt that if the heat inside his body didn't subside, he wouldn't be able to breathe much longer.

Drive faster. Drive faster, he told himself, and the air will cool you down. He floored the accelerator and the little car jumped forward, then settled into a blur of speed. Still, the air that whistled past the car felt hot and dry on Adragon's skin, and he was overcome by a terrible thirst.

The heat persevered. It felt as if the inside of the car was on fire, and Adragon took his hands off the wheel to touch his arms and his chest, but there was no flame that he could extinguish with his hands. It was inside of him, flowing through his veins.

There was another source of heat though, and that one he could do something about. He unzipped his pants, laid his hand in his lap, and his engorged penis rose to meet it. He moved his hand, and the thing came alive, jumping and throbbing with desire. He was preparing to turn off the main road onto the next side street and find a deserted spot to seek some relief, when the first flake struck his forehead.

"It's snowing," he shouted, and caught the attention of a motorist waiting at the light, which Adragon ran without looking in either direction. He waved a naked arm at the man as he passed and was rewarded by a smile of recognition, acknowledgment by a fellow nut case.

He was still waving his arm when he noticed a patrol car in the parking lot of a 7-Eleven. The cop was drinking from a styrofoam cup, and watching the road with what appeared to be halfhearted interest. Adragon lowered his arm and hunched down on the leather seat, which suddenly began to feel cold to his skin. He knew that if the cop pulled him over, he would end up at the local police station trying to explain his weird behavior, waiting for Elsbeth or Del to bail him out. Driving down the shore in a convertible, naked to the waist in a snowstorm in the dead of winter with his pants unzipped—even in this part of the country, that might be considered weird.

He shivered a little as he drove the last couple of miles. "Coming down," he muttered to himself, "crashing."

He left his shirt and jacket in the car and raced up the stairs, shunning the elevator and any inquisitive tenants who might be using it. The door to Del's condo was open, and she was waiting for him just inside. In a way, that was a disappointment because he had been envisioning himself breaking down the door and chasing her through the apartment. It was kind of anticlimactic, her just standing there with her hands on her hips, as though she had been expecting him.

But he made the best of the situation: he slapped her across the face with his open hand. The shocked look on her face and the sudden fear in her eyes was wonderful.

"Adragon, what the hell's the matter? I saw your car, and I left the door open for you, but why—"

"Shut up!" he shouted, backhanding her across the other side of her face.

"Why?" she asked. "What did I do?" and that was the last thing he let her say.

"Bitch!" he hissed, as he kicked out at her, and she squealed in pain as his boot struck her in the bottom of the stomach and doubled her over.

"Whore!" he yelled, taking a flying leap at her, which she was able to sidestep in spite of her pain and confusion.

160

"Slut!" He shoved her hard, and she stumbled backward. He saw that she was going to hit the glass-topped table with the back of her legs but he didn't move to catch her. He let her fall, and watched calmly as she toppled, her arms flailing. The glass shattered, there was a splash of crimson, and Del screamed shrilly. Her head and shoulders struck the couch, her legs landed on the table, then her body crumbled and she slid to the floor between the two pieces of furniture.

Adragon leaped to her side. For a moment, he considered lifting her carefully and carrying her to her bed. As suddenly, the thought was gone.

Blood was running in a steady stream from a jagged hole in her right calf, and the coursing red liquid drew Adragon like a magnet. He pushed the heavy table aside and knelt beside the woman he had professed to love. She seemed to be in shock; she was murmuring unintelligibly and staring at the ceiling, oblivious to Adragon's face only inches in front of her.

She didn't show any reaction when he stroked her damaged leg and lifted his bloody hand to his mouth. He licked the dripping crimson fluid from his fingers and closed his eyes as relief washed through his body. His body temperature, which had been racing up and down irradically, felt as if it was leveling off. He leaned over Del and twisted her leg so that his mouth could find the wound. She groaned in pain, and he felt a momentary pang of pity for her, but it wasn't enough to stop him.

When he had drunk his fill, he collapsed on top of Del and kissed her on her lips, which were cold and unresponsive. He tried for a minute to bring her around, but she seemed to have passed out, and Adragon was too tired to worry about it. He rolled off her and fell asleep on the floor, his face close to hers. When he woke up, the room was dark, and he was alone.

He rolled over and sat up, amazed at yet another vampire advantage: he could see perfectly in the pitch-black room. What he saw, however, didn't either amaze or please him. The room looked as if it was the site of a massacre; the white carpet was soaked with drying blood, which brought the horror of what had recently occurred in the room back to Adragon full force.

He stood shakily and felt a wave of nausea rise up from his stomach, which was empty except for the greasy egg mixture he had eaten to please Elsbeth. He stumbled to the bathroom and hung over the bowl, retching violently until he got rid of the offending eggs. Are vampires supposed to throw up? he wondered, but it wasn't a valid question, was it? In the kitchen, he groped in the refrigerator for the tiny bottle of insulin and found his needles behind a cabinet door. He prepared an injection and swabbed his upper arm with alcohol.

After he had injected himself, he walked back through the apartment, searching for Del. Her bed looked as if it hadn't been slept in, but there were drops of her ruby-red blood on the carpet in the hallway, and on the bathroom floor.

Panic drove him through the apartment, opening doors, peering into dark corners, begging her to be there. Finally, he focused in on the closet where she stored her luggage. It was still there, and Adragon breathed a sigh of relief before he realized that it was, after all, Del's home, not his. If anyone was forced to leave, it should not be Del.

Still, he walked the floor for hours, sick with the

fear that she had left him. He was unclear as to who he could call, where he could search. He knew few of her friends or acquaintances; she led, he discovered with dismay, another life quite separate from the life she shared with him.

When he heard her key in the lock, he raced to the door and pulled it open so quickly that he almost pulled her off her feet. Her face stopped the flow of words that raced to his lips.

"Del, where have you been? Why have you tortured me like this?"

To say that she was pale would have been a ridiculous understatement. Her face was bleached, prison-white, the color of snow. Her skin was translucent, and Adragon imagined that her veins were filled with a milky substance that had replaced her blood. She was a bloodless vampire, a caricature of herself. Her lips were waxen; her only hint of color was the pale blue that clouded the whites of her eyes.

But that wasn't the worst thing Adragon noticed about the woman he had savaged in a fit of vampire lust. He watched Del walk across the living room, and his breath caught in his throat. Her leg was wrapped in a white bandage, and she was limping slightly as she crossed the room, pointedly avoiding the splashes of red on the carpet.

"Oh, my God." He expelled the breath he had been holding and reached out to steady her.

"Don't touch me!" Del's voice echoed in the cavernous room, and Adragon took a step backward. "Don't touch me," she repeated, "or I won't be responsible for my actions."

Adragon spread his arms and lifted his hands to indicate that he was following her orders.

"I want you out of here, Adragon." Her voice broke

163

and she buried her face in her hands. By the time Adragon reached her side, she was sobbing. She let him touch her face, then wrap his arms around her. She collapsed against him, and he felt an outpouring of warmth for her from someplace deep inside of him where the Vampire Adragon did not yet rule.

"Del, can you ever forgive me? Here, come over to the couch and sit down."

"Not the couch, no." She cringed and he remembered too late the blood that covered the carpeting there.

He eased her gently into a huge white leather chair, and sank to his knees in front of her. "I'll clean up this mess, and take care of having the table repaired," he promised, although he knew that would be doing much too little too late.

"I'll do anything if you'll just forgive me," he went on, "I don't know what happened. No, that's not true — I do know. It was Elsbeth, she made me crazy, Del, and I took my craziness out on you."

"I forgive you." She smiled wanly, and he felt a stab of fear for her. Lifting her in his arms, he carried her to the bedroom, undressed her gently, and tucked her under the sheets in the big, warm bed. He rubbed her hands and kissed her cheeks until some color returned to her face, all the time replaying footage in his head of a struggle, a fall, a mad half-man who ripped at his lover's flesh to drink her blood.

"How do you do it?" he asked on the verge of sleep. "How do you go without blood for so long? Why doesn't the denial make you crazy?"

"I don't do without, Adragon."

"Where do you get it?" he asked, suddenly wide awake, and interested in her answer.

"The Society . . . and other places."

"Why can't you tell me? Why can't you share it with me?"

"I will when you've proven yourself."

"What do you mean 'proven yourself'?" He had to fight down his anger, to keep it from rising up and taking him over again.

"Can't talk," she mumbled, "too sleepy," and the human side of him, the boy he had been when he fell in love with her, let her sleep.

Chapter Seventeen

He heard them first, even though they were talking in whispers. Their voices carried to him on the wind, above the sound of the waves that crashed onto the shore and washed up close to the circle of men. When he first saw them, they were still several hundred feet in front of him, a small knot of humans bent over something that lay on the sand at their feet.

Adragon ran on, although he had little desire to join the group. The man who turned to welcome him to their circle was young, blond, and well-muscled, a surfer, whose gear had been abandoned several feet away. The man's straight teeth were blindingly white in his winter-tan face, but he wasn't smiling when he turned to Adragon.

"You live around here?" he asked.

"Just up the beach," Adragon answered, as he bent over and tried to catch his breath.

"You know most of your neighbors?"

"I know some of them, why?"

Adragon was tiring of the game, and he wanted to know what was going on. He couldn't see the thing that was obviously the subject of their attention; it was hidden by the men's legs, but from the grim set of the surfer's jaw, it wasn't good. Then the man who had been questioning him stepped aside, and Adragon saw her, or what was left of her.

Her thin jacket was soggy, the blouse almost completely gone, her small breasts rotting away from her breastbone. Adragon didn't want to look at her face. He didn't want to, but he did. She stared up at him with empty eye sockets under a skinless brow, through ropy strands of dark hair.

Adragon straightened and pushed through the several men who had gathered around him to watch his reaction.

"You know her?" his interrogator asked. "You know where she lived?"

But Adragon shoved the man aside and took off running up the beach, ignoring the shouts and calls that followed him.

He read about it in the next day's *Press*, and it seemed less than real: unidentified body, early twenties, foul play possible. He connected the prostitute's murder—since it would have been worse to think of her as a suicide—to the bloody needles that had recently washed up on the shore near Elsbeth's house. A coincidence? A thought kept nagging at his brain but he wouldn't entertain it. Could Elsbeth have followed him the night he went to Asbury Park and found the prostitute? Could she have been so insanely jealous?

He denied that option, but he had a hard time putting the girl's face out of his mind. That wasn't his only problem. He seemed to be losing control of every aspect of his young life.

* * *

"I don't want a donor, damn it, I want you." Adragon couldn't slow the rapid-fire hammering of his heart, or the drool that dripped from his chin when he thought of having her. Humiliated, he swept his arm across the dresser and scattered her makeup, jars and bottles and tubes of red lipstick. He walked through them, hearing them crackle and break under his weight.

Del laid her hand gently on his arm and tried to placate him. "I told you that I can't satisfy your thirst tonight, Adragon. I have another obligation."

"You said you loved me," he whined in the little-boy voice that grated on his nerves even as he used it to get his own way.

"I do love you, sweet Adragon, but I had a life before I met you and I can't just change my life completely overnight."

"I don't want you to give your blood to anyone else. I won't let you. And I don't want those damned donors. Call them and tell them not to come. I hate their damned bitter blood."

Del stood there in front of him, her face stark white, her dressing gown the color of dried blood. She stared at him silently until he settled down, then she let him draw her into his arms.

"I want your sweet blood, Del. I need your sweet blood."

"I wish I could give you what you want, my darling, but I can't. Choose one of the donors and sate yourself with their blood and their sex, if you desire it."

"You're sure they're safe?" It was obvious that he wasn't going to get his way with Del, and at least the donors were attractive, desirable young women.

"We have a doctor who checks their blood bi-weekly," Del assured him. "If they desire to be donors for us, they have to have the tests. If they miss a test, they're out, no matter how good their excuses are."

"Why isn't their blood sweet like yours?" he mumbled between planting kisses on Del's neck. He didn't really expect an answer, but he got one.

"You're a smart boy. I'd think you would have figured it out by now."

"I don't have a clue."

"I was born with diabetes, Adragon, the same as you. My vampirism has shielded me from the life-threatening side effects of the disease but my sugar level is still high and my blood is still sweet."

Adragon released Del and stepped back, to get a better view of her face.

"Are you serious?" he asked. "You can't be serious."

"There are so many things I haven't told you, so much that you have to know."

"You're telling me that my blood tastes good because I'm a diabetic? That's the craziest thing I ever heard."

Del nodded and turned back to the mirror to apply her makeup.

"And that's why I enjoy your blood," Adragon asked, staring at the reflection of her gorgeous face, "because you're diabetic?"

Her luminous green eyes met his in the mirror as she nodded to acknowledge that everything he said was true.

"That's incredible."

"Yes, it is, isn't it?"

169

She smiled up at him with her freshly painted lips, and he wanted nothing more than to keep her there with him, but he knew better than to insist.

"Wherever you're going," he said, "you'll be the most beautiful woman there." He bent quickly to kiss her neck and she stiffened before she relaxed under his lips. Adragon didn't proudly acknowledge that it gave him pleasure to know that he had the power to frighten her.

Adragon tried to lay down the law and tell her that she couldn't go, but the reality was that he was only a boy of seventeen, vampire or not. On the other hand, Del was a grown woman of twenty-six, who owned her own business, and was used to being her own boss.

"I don't want you to go," he ordered, but the words sounded ridiculous to his own ears. "Please," he added, but it didn't help much.

The meeting of the Society of Vampires was being held at 9:00 P.M. on the third Friday of the New Year. Adragon dreaded being alone, and didn't look forward to a long, boring evening either reading or watching TV. He wasn't yet too wise in the ways of vampirism, and he wasn't sure just what vampires were supposed to do with themselves when they were alone.

To be perfectly honest with himself, he was afraid of being alone. He remembered things, snatches of things from the first weeks of his awakening: the prostitutes, and the times he had attacked Del and the donors and tried to drain their blood. He didn't trust himself, and he wanted to ask her to lock him in, so that he wouldn't do anything foolish while she was gone. But, of course, he couldn't do that.

Adragon watched as Del slithered into a sequined red dress and draped a strand of pearls around her slender white neck. He stared at her neck until she turned her back to him to finish applying her makeup: white powder on her pale cheeks, red lipstick to paint a pout on her colorless lips.

She was beautiful, her body was long and slender, her hair lustrous, her face perfection. Adragon looked at her legs as she stepped into high-heeled red pumps and removed a long black cape from her closet. Her leg had healed without a scar. He took it from her and draped it over her shoulders, letting his hands slide beneath it, loving the feel of her body, its heat under the crimson dress.

Del turned to him and smiled, exposing sharp white teeth. Adragon would have sworn he saw blood welling up in her mouth and dripping down her chin, but when he blinked and looked again, her face was smooth and powder dry.

She was too perfect, that's what drove him around the bend. If there had been the slightest blemish, the smallest run in a stocking, the most minute stain or smear anywhere, he might have let her go.

He grabbed the top of the dress, which was cut low across her milky breasts, and ripped it down the front. He knew from the look on her face that she saw it coming just seconds before it happened, seconds too late. After the dress was torn, she tried to run, but he held her arms in an iron grip as she struggled against him. Trying to scream was her next mistake; he clamped his hand over her mouth and exerted pressure until she grew limp. She stopped fighting him then, as if what he was

171

doing to her didn't really matter. He worked methodically, misused her body, smeared her make-up and tangled her hair, then he left her to repair the damage.

He collapsed on her bed, and within seconds he had passed out, a victim of his own violence. He woke up what must have been hours later, and felt around in the bed for Del before he remembered what had happened. He sat up in bed and checked out the bedroom. The windows were black, it was obviously the middle of the night, and Del was not in the room. Cursing, he roamed through the apartment, until he was convinced that she was gone.

Back in the bedroom, fully awake now, he discovered the torn red dress on the floor of her closet. She had so many clothes that he couldn't begin to guess what might be missing, but he couldn't find the black cape anywhere. So, Del had obviously gone off to meet with the Society of Vampires in spite of what he had done to try and discourage her.

Trembling with rage, Adragon dialed his mother's number on the cordless phone as he paced through the house. If she was home, he was determined that he would race over there and make her take him to Del. What did he care if she got in trouble with the Society for disclosing their secret meeting place? He let the phone ring a dozen times before he threw it across the room and stalked to the kitchen for a six-pack of Coors.

He popped a can and stood at the windows in the living room to drink it, his eyes fixed on the black sea. He was surprised by a wave of almost painful homesickness, of longing for the old life that seemed to have been snatched away from him so cruelly. He was further surprised that his anger centered on Del rather than on Elsbeth, and that the more beer he drank, the more his anger changed to self-pity.

When he looked at his watch, he was surprised to see that it was the middle of the night, and Del still wasn't home. He continued to sit in front of the window, until he fell over onto the floor and passed out from sheer exhaustion.

The next day was bad, but the second day was worse. Before she left, Del had been feeding Adragon minute amounts of blood taken from the donors, and he had been taking her blood more and more often. He missed her companionship and the great sex he had with her, but mostly he missed her blood.

He knew where she kept the donor's blood, and on this second day of her absence from the apartment, he knew that he would have to dip into the supply. In the living room, there was a custom-built wall unit with a locked door on the top left section. Behind the door, there was a recessed bar, complete with a tiny refrigerated section which could be turned on high to keep ice cubes from melting during the course of a party. But there were no ice cubes in the little tray; there was blood there, and Adragon wanted it.

He wasn't supposed to know that the key was in Del's jewelry box, but he had watched her hide it after she refilled the empty vials after the donors' last visit. He thought it would be easy to take the key from its hiding place under her earring tray and use it to unlock the door to the cabinet which held the blood.

The key wasn't where it was supposed to be, and Adragon swept the jewelry box from the top of Del's dresser, scattering gold and silver to all corners of the bedroom.

Back in the living room, he grabbed the brass ring on the bar door and pulled hard. The lock held. He jiggled the door back and forth, took out his pocket knife and fiddled with the lock. Nothing happened. The simple little door was locked up tight and unless he felt like smashing it, Adragon was out of luck.

He kicked the wall unit viciously, grabbed his leather jacket, and left the apartment. He wasn't dressed for running on the beach, so he walked across the damp sand and felt it seep inside his leather running shoes and wet the bottom of his jeans. He zipped his jacket and stood at the edge of the water, as the rising tide lapped at his feet.

He needed blood, felt the need pounding in his head. He was weak and cold, nauseous, and he needed Del to help him. But Del was gone, Del had left him, and he had no idea how to find her. After a long time, he noticed that his shoes were covered with water, and he started back to the condo. In the lobby, he heard an unfamiliar noise, a low, mewling sound. He pinpointed it as coming from behind the couch, and leaning over the back, spotted the kitten. His blood thudded in his temples and he imagined that he could see past the animal's furry gray and black stripes to where its blood flowed through its tiny veins. It wasn't human blood but it would

174

do, it would keep something bad from happening to him until Del came back to help him.

On his knees, Adragon made clucking noises with his tongue and called "kitty, kitty" to lure the animal out from behind the couch. It came gladly, anxious for a human touch and the possibility of a meal to fill its empty belly. Adragon scooped it up and tucked it under his jacket where he could feel its heart pumping against his own. He retraced his steps to the privacy of the deserted parking lot behind the condo complex.

Growing up, Adragon was a gentle boy who had never intentionally hurt anyone or anything. But now that he was a vampire, everything was different. It was an act against his own nature when he twisted the kitten's head until he heard its neck snap, a worse sound than he would ever have imagined. He stood holding it while its green eyes stared up at him, as blood and spittle ran from its nose and mouth. Its body grew limp in his hands, and he was totally grossed out, close to losing what little food he had consumed over the past two days.

Adragon couldn't stop, and he didn't try to rationalize what he was doing. He quickly slit the kitten's furry throat with his pocket knife and, shaking with thirst, sank his teeth into the cavity and ripped the skin away. He sucked the bitter animal blood into his mouth and nose, choked, spit, and splashed the front of his jacket with gore. He lifted the body above his head and let the viscous red liquid drip into his mouth. His teeth were sensitive; they ached as the warm blood washed over them. His tongue became coated, thick and foreign in his mouth. In spite of his disgust, Adragon reveled in the wonder

175

of his lone ritual, and sent thanks to whatever Power had blessed him with the priceless gift of Vampirism.

The animal was quickly drained of blood, and Adragon's euphoric feelings passed. He was left with an emptiness, with a sensation too much like human hunger in his belly. He grimaced, with the thought that his stomach felt much like it felt two or three hours after a generous restaurant meal, when he began to wish that he had taken his leftovers in a doggy bag. The animal blood had been a panacea, nothing more. What he needed was human blood, and he would not be able to last through the night without it.

He threw the cat in the trash, swiped at the blood on his jacket, and strode back into the lobby. Luck was with him; the lobby was empty, the elevator waiting. Upstairs, he threw his clothes, including his jacket, in the trash. He was in the shower, lathering his body with a bar of Irish Spring, when the shower doors opened and Del stepped inside. Taking the soap out of his hand, she used it to caress his shoulders, his back, his buttocks.

"You're smiling," Del teased, "what have you been up to?"

"I've been out doing vampire things; what have you been doing?"

"Sleeping, you nut, it's the middle of the night. Seriously, Adragon—"

"No," he answered, and covered her lips with his to stop her questions. Del was back, that was all that mattered.

He didn't realize that he had been hallucinating until he went in search of her the following morning. The apartment was empty, the bedroom floor was a shambles of broken bottles and jars, and Del was not there. It took Adragon a long time to reconcile himself to the fact that Del had not come home, and that his mind was playing tricks on him. He wondered how long he would be able to exist without her.

Chapter Eighteen

By the end of that day, Adragon knew that he couldn't be alone any longer. One more night spent avoiding the big bed where he and Del had so often made love would surely be his undoing.

He waited until the sun set, until his blood felt as if it was thinning, his heart slowing down. Until he felt the need, the awful thirst come upon him.

He ran from the condo without stopping to find a jacket, without realizing where he was going. But within a half hour, he was there, hammering on the door, calling out to her.

"Mommy?" The voice was reedy and thin, unrecognizable to Adragon. He heard it but didn't identify with its source.

He pounded harder, and the wind rose from the ocean to wrap itself around his body and shake him gently back and forth. Elsbeth's car was parked under the house, so he knew that she was home, unless someone else had picked her up and driven her to the meeting. She had to be home. He pounded again, picturing her asleep in her huge, comfortable bed, dreaming bloodred dreams.

"Mommy, please . . ." The voice was not his own but it issued from his mouth. He struck the window beside the door with the palm of his hand, but it didn't make enough noise to awaken his mother. The sound it made was dull and hollow, and it hurt his hand, but the house remained dark and silent. She was never going to come, was she?

"MOMMY!" The scream tore from his throat and brought the taste of his own blood to his lips.

He was crying when Elsbeth opened the door and drew him into the warmth of her house, into the comfort of her arms.

"Oh, Adragon," was all she said when she finally moved back and looked into his troubled eyes.

"I've missed you, Mommy. I want to come home. Can I come home now?"

By way of answer, she led him to his room and turned down the bed while he waited, standing as close to her as he could. She helped him undress and tucked him into bed, and he had never felt so grateful to anyone for anything.

"She's gone, and I'm so thirsty, Mommy," he whined. "I'm afraid of everything, I don't trust my-self."

"I know, dear. Just lie back and sleep, I'm going to take care of you. You're home now, my dear Adragon, and you will never have to be alone again."

"Thirsty . . ." he whimpered, then watched in awe as Elsbeth unbuttoned her silk robe and let it slide from her shoulders. Even in his present state of con-fusion, there was a spark of curiosity as he wondered what his mother was going to do.

She went away for a few seconds, then returned to kneel beside his bed. There was a red mark on her neck just beneath her ear, a rather deep-looking cut that was starting to bleed. As Adragon watched in

179

fascination, red liquid seeped from the cut and ran down her neck, faster. He traced the path of his mother's blood with his eyes as it ran in pink rivulets across the swell of her breasts and reddened the top of her white nightgown.

"Drink," she offered, but he could only stare at her in disbelief. Finally, her small hands touched his temples and drew his mouth to the wound in her throat.

"Drink," she commanded, and still Adragon tried to resist. He whimpered and whined and turned his head away, but the smell of blood was so strong in his nostrils that it quickly overpowered him. When she offered her neck to him again, his response was that of a baby hungry for his mother's milk. He gobbled and sucked at her neck with a passion beyond his control until she pinched his ear to stop him, then pushed him away from her and held him until he had calmed down sufficiently for her to let him go.

Minutes later, she let him drink again for a minute or two before she left him to close her wound and clean herself up. When she came back with a wet washcloth to cleanse his face, he turned his back to her and mumbled "Sleepy," then fell asleep with a smile on his face.

"How are you feeling?" Elsbeth asked when Adragon staggered into the kitchen several hours later.

"Dizzy," he mumbled, not looking her in the eye, "and foolish as hell."

"Forget that." Elsbeth sat a bowl of steaming hot

180

cereal on the table and motioned for him to sit down. "Every boy is entitled to need his mo—"

"Don't say it, okay?"

"His mother, that's all I was going to say. Every boy is entitled to need his mother once in a while, no matter how old he is."

"Let's just forget it."

She shrugged her slim shoulders, elegant in a royal blue caftan, and Adragon couldn't help but notice the rise and fall of her small breasts under the embroidered silk. It boggled his mind to think that this small woman had conceived him, carried him for nine months, and brought him into the world. She was so tiny, so frail, and surely not old enough to be his mother.

"What?" she asked, and he quickly lowered his eyes from her breasts to her hands, which were resting on the back of a kitchen chair as she stood across the table from him.

"Us," he finally answered when it became evident that she would wait for an answer. "We've done just about everything together, haven't we?"

"Just about," she answered, and let a smile flirt with the corners of her mouth. Then her eyes clouded over and Adragon stood and reached across the table to lay his hands on top of hers.

"Don't leave me," he pleaded, "take me with you again."

"I can't, don't you understand? I was too indulgent, I traced the routes for you, but now you have to travel them alone."

He shook his head and struggled with a feeling of deep sadness. "I don't remember the way," he admitted.

181

"It will come back to you, Adragon. You've been there so many times before. The way is deep within yourself."

"I'm not as strong as you are, or as sure of myself."

Her laughter filled the room and escaped through the kitchen window that she cracked to air out the house. When she turned back, she had sobered, and she drew him to her with the strange power she held over him.

"You have drunk the blood of kings," she whispered, "you are invincible."

Elsbeth loved drama, and she often exaggerated, but this time Adragon knew his mother spoke the truth.

He listened intently, as she continued to instruct him. "When things got bad, we could always stop our hearts and go back to the other place. That was our only defense against a stake through the heart, or being buried alive. We always had the last laugh, Adragon. The fools would chase us down like animals, corner us, and mete out the worst punishment their unimaginative little minds could come up with to rid themselves of the threat of our existence."

"But what happened?" Adragon asked when Elsbeth stopped to catch her breath. "Why didn't it work in our last incarnation? Did you leave without me?"

"Something happened," she said, her voice so low that he had to move closer to catch her words, "something so terrible that we could not reconcile during that lifetime."

"What? What happened?" he insisted. "You remember, I know you do."

182

"I don't remember." She looked him straight in the eye when she said it, and he knew that she was lying.

"But you remember so much. You remember things that happened hundreds of years ago."

"Our long-range memories are selective. Otherwise, we couldn't deal with the flood of memories. We pick and choose what we *want* to remember."

"Why don't you want to remember it, Elsbeth? What did you do to me that was so terrible that you've chosen to lock it out of your conscious mind forever?"

"My, aren't we dramatic tonight! What makes you so sure that it was I who did something to you?"

"Just a hunch, Mother dear."

She locked his eyes with hers and searched his heart, looking for any further knowledge that he might be trying to hide from her. When she saw that he knew nothing other than what he had already mentioned, she smiled and broke eye contact.

"God, you're good, Elsbeth."

"I don't know what happened in that last lifetime, Adragon," she continued as if their original conversation had never been interrupted, "but you didn't come back with me. I waited for you all through my childhood, longing for you, needing you. When you didn't come, I married, thinking that I might never see you again. Then I conceived a child, and I knew immediately that the soul was yours. I felt your presence in my womb, growing, feeding off my own flesh and blood. And I fed you gladly. I would have let you eat my heart to keep you alive. I knew you would be a boy, and I chose your name with care. Adragon, Adragon Hart."

183

It was a weird experience, having his own name spoken so reverently in the quiet room, as if it were a prayer.

"The minute you were born," Elsbeth continued, "I lost all interest in your father. I ignored him, and spent all of my time with you. You were the most beautiful baby in the world. I would sit for hours just staring at your face, looking into your eyes and through them into your soul."

"But why didn't you—"

"Why didn't I tell you what you were? That you were my soul mate, my lover? You must trust me when I say that there were reasons, and that some-day you will learn of them, when the time is right."

Elsbeth roasted a chicken for their dinner, and Adragon realized how much he had missed his mother's cooking. Del's culinary talents were limited to finding delicatessens that had passable take-out food. Elsbeth served herself a small portion, but she paid little attention to what was on her plate. He felt her eyes on him as he tasted the delicious stir-fry vegetables she had prepared especially for him. He ate heartily, in spite of the fact that she made him nervous, watching him as if they were lovers, as if the meal they shared was only the beginning of their evening's enjoyment.

"I'll help you clean up," he offered as they sipped their after-dinner coffee, but she wouldn't hear of it.

"You'll spoil me, Mother."

"I want to." Such a simple statement, why did he read more into it? *I'll spoil you, so that you'll never want to leave me again.*

184

She didn't offer him any blood that night, and Adragon wasn't surprised. He had been taught by both Del and Elsbeth that a vampire's needs were simple, that a vampire should not be greedy, and he had drunk his fill the night before. The memory of drinking his mother's blood still embarrassed him, and he felt his face flush as he pictured her pale neck and the way he had nuzzled at her flesh like a greedy newborn baby.

Adragon changed into a warm jogging suit and went out into the night while Elsbeth puttered in the kitchen. The smooth black sea beckoned to him, and he ran up the beach until he was almost too exhausted to retrace his steps. For some reason, he expected to see Raymond on the beach that night, and the man didn't disappoint him.

"Adragon, you're looking fit, my boy."

"You're looking pretty good yourself, Ray." It was true, the man seemed to grow younger instead of older each time Adragon saw him.

"Listen, Ray, about that day up at the house—"

"We won't talk about that day, my boy." The man waved away Adragon's protest and walked along beside him. "Have I ever told you that I envy you these late-night runs? Well, I do. I'm afraid my exercise level is low, at best, but you—you run like the wind."

"I don't do it every night like I used to, I'm kind of out of shape now," Adragon answered, wondering how many times Raymond had watched him run without revealing himself.

"You, out of shape? Hardly," Raymond laughed.

The old guy was sharp, Adragon had to give him credit. Actually, he had only said that he was out of shape to see what Raymond would say in return. He had to admit to himself that he kind of resented the older man's constant intrusion into his life and Elsbeth's.

"Well, it's past my bedtime, but I'll no doubt see you tomorrow night. My best to Elsbeth."

"Sure, Ray." The man probably didn't intend any harm, but there it was again, the interference, the "See you tomorrow night." "Not if I can help it," Adragon mumbled to himself when the man was out of earshot, "not if I see you first."

Raymond wasn't the only one watching Adragon's every move. "Was that Raymond you were talking to on the beach last night?" Elsbeth asked over coffee the next morning.

"Yeah. For someone who swears he hates exercise, he stays in pretty good shape for a guy his age, doesn't he?"

Elsbeth didn't answer and when Adragon looked at her and waited for a reply, she mumbled something that sounded like "I guess so."

"You know something strange, Mother?"

"No, but I'm sure you're going to tell me."

"You're right, I am. He didn't seem to be surprised that I was here, didn't even ask me about it."

"Raymond is a very private person, and he respects other people's privacy in return for their respect of his."

"You think that's it?"

"Definitely."

"You're probably right. But then, you're always right, Elsbeth, that's what's so damned infuriating about you."

She smiled, kissed his cheek and retreated to her

office, leaving Adragon alone with the questions she hadn't quite answered.

Being separated from Del was like an illness, a disease that never stopped causing him pain. He enjoyed being home, in the first and only home he had ever known. He thrived on his mother's attention, listened for the sound of her voice, loved watching her work. He sat on the studio couch in her office, his back to the crashing ocean waves, his legs folded under him. A computer magazine was open on the couch beside him, and every once in a while he turned a page, but they both knew that his eyes were on Elsbeth's profile as she bent over her keyboard. Her forehead creased in thought, her eyes narrowed, the tip of her tongue protruded from her mouth and caressed her upper lip as her characters came to life on the green and black screen.

Adragon felt content, surrounded by warmth and affection, as though this was where he belonged. If only Del could be here with him. If only.

"My safe harbor," he murmured to himself and only realized that he had spoken aloud when Elsbeth broke from her work to turn and smile at him.

"I want to show you something, Adragon." It was hours later and she had finished working for the day. She was too tired to bother with cooking, and they were waiting for a delivery from a local Italian restaurant. She was letting Adragon go off his diabetic diet for the evening, and she considered that a real indulgence, even though he told her he no longer followed it to the letter.

Elsbeth left the room for several seconds and returned carrying an old brown leather album. "Oh, photographs," he said, not even trying to hide his boredom.

"Just one. I'm sure you've seen it a hundred times, but tonight it will look different to you."

"Let me see."

She opened the album and placed it in front of him, pointing with a crimson fingernail to the picture she referred to.

"You were six, you can't possibly remember."

"No, I don't." He shook his head, puzzled as to why she wanted him to look at that particular photograph.

"Just before I snapped the picture, I asked you what you wanted to be when you grew up, and do you know what you said?"

"No, but I'll bet it was good."

"You said you wanted to be a vampire."

"Did I say 'just like you, Mom?' "

"I gave you red Kool-Aid and you pretended that it was blood."

"You're making this up."

"I'm not, truly."

"Well, what's the point, should I get all choked up about this or something?"

"You're not a sentimental person, are you, Adragon?"

"Hell, no, and neither are you, Elsbeth."

"You're right." She slammed the album shut and tossed it across the room.

"Come and get your vampire blood, my vampire son," she teased, crooking a finger at him and slithering out of the room. Adragon hated himself for following her, but he did.

In her bedroom, which was like a foreign country to Adragon, since he had spent so little time there, Elsbeth began to make preparations. She assembled a thirsty bath towel, alcohol swabs, and the sharp instrument she would use to prick her own skin, or his. She removed a sexy white nightgown from a drawer but before she could make a move to change into it, Adragon caught her by the arm and pulled her over to the bed.

"I want to talk first," he said, needing time to prepare himself for what was about to happen.

Elsbeth looked at him with new respect, and that made it easier. "Go ahead," she said, "ask me whatever it is."

"We've never been apart, not in all the hundreds of years?"

"Does that matter?"

"Yes, it matters a lot. I wonder about Del, about us."

"You aren't destined to be my lover in this lifetime, Adragon, if that's what you're getting at. But that doesn't mean that I want to let go of you either. We can be together, as mother and son."

"That's not a natural relationship, Elsbeth. I mean, it was while I was growing up, but I'm a grown man now."

"You're seventeen years old, Adragon, and you need me. Maybe someday you'll be able to survive without me, but not today. Not tonight." She started to rise, but he held onto her.

"If I died, would you stop your own heart so that you could go with me, Elsbeth?"

"You are my heart, Adragon, my heart and my soul."

She rose from the bed and Adragon spoke sharply, "Don't put that nightgown on, okay?"

"Not put it on? Surely you don't want me naked," she teased.

"Just stay the way you are."

She glanced down at her one-piece jumpsuit and smiled indulgently. "I have nothing on under this, darling, and the neck is too high to pull down. Any other suggestions?"

When Adragon shook his head, she continued to the bathroom and returned several minutes later wearing the white nightgown. It was made of some thin, satiny material, and barely covered her nipples.

She tossed the bed pillows to the floor and laid down across the bed, staring up at her son with her startling blue eyes. She was trying to look innocent, but Adragon knew that she was anything but that. "Are you ready?" she asked, and he acknowledged that he was.

Using the small, sharp instrument that seemed to be a mainstay of every vampire's bag of tricks, she drew a line about three-quarters of an inch long on her chest wall, just where the swell of her breasts began. The skin puffed out around the incision, and Adragon turned his head away, feeling as if he might lose his dinner any minute. When he looked back, the skin on Elsbeth's chest appeared to be intact, and he breathed easier. Then a tiny crimson bubble appeared, and soon there were a dozen drops of blood, then a steady stream of it flowing down Elsbeth's side onto the towel she had placed on the bed beneath her upper body.

"Drink," she ordered, then closed her eyes and waited for him to begin.

190

He laid one hand gently on her breast, the other on her collarbone, his dark curly hair fell onto her chest as he bent over her. He caught her blood on his tongue as it left the wound. She guided his face with her hands so that he wouldn't fear to lick the tracks it left as it ran in lazy rivers and formed a tiny lake in the hollow of her breasts.

She said "Enough," and he stopped although the desire to continue was almost overwhelming. As he pushed himself away from her, his hand brushed her nipple and he mumbled an apology, sick with shame. He rose without looking at her, and stumbled out of the room, drunk on his mother's blood.

Adragon fell into his bed and slept soundly for several hours, his dreams a black pit from which he could not emerge. When he woke up, he immediately thought of Del, and spent the rest of the night awake, missing her. He needed to talk to her, because who else in the world would listen to his wild fears, his ridiculous accusations?

He had heard of such things happening, of a mother clinging to her son, doing everything within her power to stop him from having a life of his own. But this was different, this was worse, because Elsbeth's hold on him wasn't for a lifetime, it was for all his lifetimes. It was forever.

Adragon walked the floor the next night until he was worn out, until his knees buckled and he fell to the couch. He sat there for hours, staring out at the sea. The tide came in, waves whipped to white froth crashed on the sand beyond the house. He watched, half-expecting to see Del walking on the waves, coming to him in a sea-green gown, her arms spread wide to greet him. Finally, he opened the door and walked out onto the balcony, into the misty night. But there was no woman there. It was the play of moonlight on the waves that had lured him out from the warmth of his mother's dwelling.

Slumped on the couch again, he willed the telephone to ring. But it didn't ring, and Del didn't come for him.

Elsbeth tended to his needs and seemed to be worried over the fact that he was neglecting to take care of himself. She took a syringe of his blood and sent it to a lab for testing, making a project out of boxing it and affixing an address label, so that he would know for sure that she wasn't drinking it. And Adragon was sure he knew why she didn't need his blood. She had the upper hand, at least temporarily, because he needed her to survive without Del, and she apparently didn't need him.

Chapter Nineteen

Del was gone for six days, and Adragon felt as if years of his life had seeped away during that period. He grew silent and lethargic, longing for Del to the very depths of his soul. Even in the glut of blood furnished to him by his mother, he could not be distracted from thoughts of Del.

He had to give Elsbeth points for trying though. She offered him her small, solid body, opened wide for his pleasure, the red blood spilling out. She encouraged him to stroke her arms and legs, to plant kisses on her white neck and her smooth, powdered cheeks.

While he sucked her blood from her chest, her stomach, her thighs, she twined her fingers in his hair and massaged his shoulders until the tension left him and he relaxed in her arms. Then she cradled him tenderly, as a mother cradles her child. She acted as if the fact that he was seventeen years old and was more a man than his father had ever been didn't matter. But Adragon knew that it did. He had never shared such a degree of intimacy with his mother before, and he felt guilty about doing it now. But he didn't stop, because he was afraid that she could cut off his supply of blood, and without Del to help him, he had no way to get in touch with the donors.

Anyway, his mother's blood was rich and thick, and he had come to savor the taste of it on his tongue. The way it coated the inside of his mouth pleased him, the way it soothed his troubled mind and let him forget about Del for even a few short minutes of the day made it indispensable to him.

The sixth night he had a dream, and it was the worst nightmare of his life. Del came to him while he slept, her beautiful face in shadow. She didn't speak or cry out, but Adragon could see the pain in her eyes. Her tears shone like beacons on the dark landscape of his dreams and beckoned him to come to her.

He woke up with his head pounding, and the room spinning wildly around him. The bedclothes were tangled around his legs, but he somehow managed to make it to the toilet before he vomited up everything in his stomach.

He took the dream to mean that she was coming back, and he took it as a warning.

Adragon was sitting in the kitchen naked to the waist and Elsbeth was massaging his back when he heard the revving of a motorcycle engine under the house. He pushed his mother out of his way, ran to the back door, and glanced out just in time to see a scroungy-looking guy of about his own age climbing the steps to the porch two at a time. Adragon grabbed his shirt from the back of his chair and stuck his arms into the sleeves before he opened the door and stepped out onto the porch. It was a cold day, with the temperature around freezing, and the ocean breeze was strong.

"Adragon," Elsbeth called out, "get back in here, you'll catch your death." She pounded on the door and made an attempt to open it, but he held onto the knob. "What's up, man?" he asked the leather-clad boy who was catching his breath at the top of the steps.

"I'm lookin' for a A-dragon Hart. You him?"

"Yeah, I'm him."

"I got a message for you from a broad — 'cuse me," the boy apologized when Adragon moved a step closer, "a *lady* named Del. You want me to — "

The boy caught the look on Adragon's face and he backed off, stumbling dangerously close to the steep staircase.

"Go on," Adragon urged, "give me the message."

"It's right here, man. It was — Someplace — "

The boy was clearly rattled, searching frantically through his pockets for the elusive message that was obviously much more important than he had thought it to be. Adragon tried to control his mounting impatience but after several long minutes, his control snapped. He grabbed the boy by the front of his jacket, lifted him off the ground, and threw him up against the porch railing.

"Where is it, damn it, where's the message?" he shouted over the sound of the breaking surf.

The kitchen door opened slowly and Elsbeth stepped out into the raw wind with Adragon's blue sweater in her outstretched hand.

"Put this on," she ordered, "it's cold out here."

Adragon plucked the sweater from her hand and tossed it over the banister.

"Get the hell out of here, Mother. This is none of your business. Go back inside. Now!"

He gave Elsbeth a shove, and she was smart enough to back off without an argument. Still, she couldn't keep her mouth shut for long. From a position of safety just inside the door, she peered out. "What is it?" she wanted to know. "What does he want?"

"Get the goddamned hell out of my face, Elsbeth," Adragon screamed, "or I'm going to slap the shit out of you."

She glared at him but she shut the door the final inch she had been holding it open and disappeared from sight.

Adragon turned back to the delivery boy, who hadn't moved from the spot where Adragon had deposited him. He had a stupid grin on his face which told Adragon that he had been watching Adragon's exchange with Elsbeth with interest.

"Now give me the fuckin' message, man, or you're dead meat."

That was all Adragon had to say to spur the boy to action. He thrust an envelope at Adragon's chest and was already on the steps when Adragon reached out for him.

"Don't you want to wait for your tip?" he asked, and the kid shook his head frantically back and forth.

Then, "Where did you get this?" Adragon asked quietly tapping the plain white envelope with a fingernail.

196

"I told you, from a woman named Del-something."

"What did she look like?"

"I don't have a clue, man, and that's the God-honest truth. It was dark, and she had this hood-thing over her head. She just gave me the note real quick-like and paid me to deliver it. I only did it for the bread, man."

"When?"

"When what?"

"When did she give you the envelope?" Adragon asked patiently.

"Last night, man, late last night, like around midnight."

Finished with him, Adragon gave the boy a shove and ignored the curses that issued from his mouth as he stumbled down the steep staircase. A shaken Adragon stood on the porch, trembling with emotion, until he heard the boy's bike start up and pull out from under the house. Then he opened the kitchen door, pushed Elsbeth out of his way, and took the mysterious missive to his bedroom.

With the door locked, he sat down on the side of the bed and slit the nondescript envelope. A sheet of typing paper fell out onto the bed. What he read was more than he had hoped for, and less.

My sweet Adragon . . . there was no way to contact you. I know you've been worrying about me. I know you've returned to your mother's house. The question now is, can you forgive me? Will you come back? Anticipating that the answer is "yes," I have one more favor to ask of you. As desperately as I need to see you, can you give me one more day alone?

197

Come to me the day after you receive this,
at the condo. I love you, sweet Adragon.

The note was signed with a big *D* and if it had
said "Come now," Adragon would have kissed the paper it was written on. But it didn't say that.

He crumpled the sheet, then flattened it out
again. His hands shook, his head reeled. He felt the
familiar tightening of his gums, the release of saliva
that heralded the awful hunger that he felt just
thinking about her. "Go to hell, Del Keelan," he
shouted to the room, but the next minute he was
down on his knees beside the bed, so grateful for the
communication from her that his legs gave out on
him.

She was asking him to give her a day, and he
knew that she would be angry with him for ignoring
her request, but there was no way that he could wait
another twenty-four hours to see her.

When he opened his door, Elsbeth was standing
on the other side, and she begged him to stop and
talk to her, but Adragon brushed past her. He
shoved his arms into the sleeves of his new brown
leather jacket as he ran.

"Adragon, don't go. Stay here with me, don't fall
for that bitch's lies. She's only using you. Adragon,
damn it, listen to me. I'm your mother, damn it!"

He kept on running and pretended that it didn't
hurt, but it did. It hurt to walk out on his mother,
especially after they had recently shared so much.
But it would have hurt worse to stay. He had no
idea where Del had been for the past six days, or
who she had been with. He only knew that she had
missed him and was reaching out to him. If she was

in trouble or in pain, he had to be there.

It wasn't until he was in the Mustang, tooling down the coast highway, that he began to fear for himself. "I am a vampire," he whispered to the night that was closing in around him but even to his own ears, his proclamation sounded weak and uncertain. There were still so many things he didn't understand. He was totally dedicated to his new lifestyle, and grateful to Del for initiating him, but there were still moments of very real, very mortal panic, and this was one of them. He had to wonder how he could possibly help Del if he had no confidence in himself.

"I am a vampire!" Adragon bellowed at the top of his lungs. He hit the horn with the heel of his hand and kept it there until the several cars in front of him on the highway pulled to the side and let him pass. He kept repeating his vow of confidence until he reached Del's condo. By that time, he was so fired up that he felt as if he could conquer the entire world for her. She had made a silent plea for his help, and he would give it.

He used his key to get into the apartment, closed the door quietly behind him, and walked through the condo in the dark. He moved silently through the living room, down the carpeted hallway, into Del's bedroom.

She was lying in bed, the blankets pulled up to her chin. The blinds were closed, the drapes drawn across the windows that looked out to the sea. Something was wrong, Adragon could feel it in the air, smell it in the room.

"Del? Are you awake? Are you okay?"

When she stirred but didn't turn over to face him,

Adragon walked around the bed and peered down at her. His eyes took a moment to adjust to the blackness of the bedroom, which was darker than the rest of the apartment. He reached toward the switch on Del's bedside lamp, but she stopped him with her voice.

"No," was all she said, but the word sent a ripple of fear through Adragon's body. He squatted beside the bed and pulled the blankets down a few inches, overcoming Del's resistance with his superior strength. Even in the dark bedroom he could see it, and his fear came rocketing back.

Del fell into his arms and clung to him, trying to hide her face in his chest, but Adragon pushed her away and hit the lamp switch. She gasped as light fell in a pool on the pillow where she was struggling to bury her face. Adragon pinned her shoulders down and turned her toward the light.

He immediately wished that he had honored her wishes and left her alone for another day. Maybe it would have been better then, maybe not. Del was a vampire, he knew that, but he had never fully accepted the reality of her vampirism or his own until that moment.

Her skin was gray, not pale or colorless, as he had seen it before, but a definite color: gray. There were uneven streaks of darker gray on her face and chest, as if even more blood had been drained away from those areas. Her lips and nails were dark, almost black. The only real color was in the whites (grays) of her eyes, which were dissected by a million tiny red lines.

He touched her lightly and found no bones intact in her face, no substance under her skin. He held

200

her chin gingerly, sure that if he applied the slightest pressure, his fingers would slide through her face and into her mouth.

Del tried her best not to meet his eyes, but Adragon insisted. When she finally turned them to him, her eyes were sunken in her face, and they held a great sadness.

"I'm not going to go away, Del," he promised. "You'll have to tell me what happened."

She started to cry softly, and Adragon welcomed her tears. At least, they proved that she was still alive and capable of emotion. When she finally stopped crying, Adragon pulled the blankets down and slid her nightgown off her shoulders. She didn't protest when he exposed her gray flesh and examined the purple bruises that covered her shoulders, chest, and upper arms. His stomach turned over when he saw the welts on her thighs and the human teeth marks on her stomach.

With more strength than he would have bet she had, Del pulled the blankets out of his grasp and covered herself.

"That's enough," she whispered, "you've seen enough to know what happened."

"Yeah, I guess I know what happened. I'd say you spent the last six days with a vampire, a mean, sadistic son of a bitch who tried to kill you but didn't quite accomplish what he set out to do. I'd say he used you in just about every perverted way his sick mind could devise, to give himself pleasure, is that about it?"

"It wasn't that way—"

"The hell it wasn't!" Adragon yelled, "But tell me how it was for you, Del. Did you enjoy it as much as he did?"

"That isn't fair, Adragon, what do you want from me?"

"You know what I want from you, damn it. I want to know if you were with him of your own free will."

Adragon grabbed her by the shoulders and shook her, forgetting how badly she was hurt until she screamed out in pain.

He took his hands off her, but he couldn't just let it go. "Answer me, Del," he insisted.

"It wasn't like that," she said again, "I did it because I had to."

"You *had* to?"

He had to ask her to repeat her reply before he was sure he'd heard her correctly.

"It was my punishment."

"Your punishment? For what, for Christ's sake? What could you possibly have done to deserve this?" He raised his arm in a gesture that took in her face and her body, all the sadistic, dehumanizing things that had been done to her.

"I can't tell you that." Adragon lifted her off the bed and threw her back down, jolting her battered body with pain.

"Stop it," she screamed, "stop it!"

And when he reached for her again, "I'm pregnant."

He didn't say anything, and she covered her eyes with her hands. He knew that she was weeping, but he couldn't find words, not for several minutes.

"It was the Society, wasn't it?" he asked finally, and she nodded that it was.

"But why would they do this to you? Didn't you

tell them that you were—"

She uncovered her eyes and looked up, anticipating his next words.

"Oh, my God. That's why they beat you—because you're pregnant. You weren't supposed to get pregnant, at least not with *my* baby. I'm right, aren't I?"

"Yes, you're right," she said after a short hesitation, "but that's all I can tell you. If you want to beat me, go ahead, then you'll be as evil as they are."

He knelt beside the bed and pulled her into his arms, no longer seeing the awful grayness. He closed his eyes and saw her beauty, the beautiful woman, and the even more beautiful soul that inhabited her body.

"I don't want to beat you," he told her gently, "I only want to love you. A baby . . ."

Chapter Twenty

In the morning light, Adragon was hardly able to look at Del. Her color was a little better, some of the grayness was gone, and her skin seemed to be more translucent than ever. He could almost see her weak, diluted blood flowing through her veins, barely keeping her body alive, and the vision frightened him.

He fed her his blood, insisted that she drink more than was safe, and wondered why in the hell he hadn't thought of feeding her the night before when she lay so gray and helpless in his arms. He made a tiny slit in a vein in his right wrist and let the precious, life-giving liquid drip into her open mouth. As the blood ran down her throat, she was forced to swallow several times in quick succession, and soon she began to move her lips, to suck at the small wound. Eventually, she opened her eyes and smiled wanly at Adragon, thanking him without words for keeping her alive.

There was no doubt in his mind that she had been close to death when he found her. Maybe the Society of Vampires, or whichever one of their members had done this to her, had not meant for her to survive. He swore to himself that he would kill the person or persons who did this to Del, if and when he discovered their identity.

He wiped the blood from her chin and she smiled at him, her lips and teeth stained crimson. "It will be all right now, sweet Adragon, I promise. It's over. Come lie with me."

She held out stick-thin arms, and he couldn't resist her, despite the fact that he knew that he should let her rest and regain her strength. Adragon laid his head on her breast and calmed her by agreeing with her that it was over, but it wasn't, and it never would be until he had his revenge. Del was goodness incarnate, and the thing that had done this to her was evil incarnate. Vampire or not, if there was a way to kill it, Adragon vowed to find that way.

He spent the day in bed with Del, nursing her back to health, satisfying his hunger with the cold, preserved blood of the donors. His intuition, human but aided by his vampire's ability to see beyond the walls of reality, warned him that he was heading full speed toward a crossroads. He felt that it would not be long before he would be forced to choose between his two natures, to abandon one for the fulfillment of the other. Beyond that moment in time, his life would be forever changed, and Del would either belong to him or be lost to him. Or she might choose to return to the man who had hurt her. If that happened, there was no doubt in Adragon's mind that he would have to kill both of them.

After that night when he discovered her drained of blood and spirit, Adragon became obsessed with Del. He swore that he would never let her go to a meeting of the Society of Vampires again.

"You don't understand, Adragon," she argued,

"if I don't go, both of us are in danger."

"I'm not afraid of them."

She laughed, and her cruelty hurt his pride.

"I'm sorry, Adragon, but you truly don't know what you're up against. Some of these people have been on earth for hundreds of years. They're brilliant, and they know things, how to make themselves invisible, how to drain the energy from the bodies of their enemies. They could kill you without leaving a clue, without touching you."

"They can't kill me, I'm a vampire, too, remember?"

"Oh, you're so naive, to think that you would be a match for them. They are the masters, the leaders, they could crush you like an ant if you tried to harm one of them."

"I don't believe you. Anyway, I don't want you to go to their meetings. You can find some excuse to stay away."

"There is no excuse, Adragon, I'm one of them, and if you want to stay with me, you'll have to accept that."

"What about the baby? Will they try to hurt the baby?"

"No, not as long as I go to the meetings and continue to stay in their good graces."

"Isn't that a stupid thing to say after what they just did to you?"

"I told you it's over now. They've forgiven me."

But Adragon didn't trust them and without alarming Del, he started getting up when her alarm went off so that he could see that she got to work safely. He showered and dressed quickly and left the condo right after she did each morning. He drove up the

206

highway, several cars behind her red Nissan and if she knew what he was doing, she didn't let on.

While Del worked in the busy boutique, selling cruise wear to spoiled society matrons, Adragon sat in a dark bar across the street and nursed a beer for hours. After a week, he admitted to himself that she had to know that he was there, and she had to know why. He followed her home when she left the shop, arriving at the condo just minutes after she did, but again, she made no reference to the fact that he had been out all day, or that the bed was unmade, the breakfast dishes still in the sink.

Del wasn't angry with him. On the contrary, since she had returned to Adragon, their lovemaking had changed for the better. It was no longer a battle of wills, a constant struggle for domination. Now they made love in a very human way, each anxious to meet the other's needs. He was gentle with her, mindful of her fragility. And Del was more than generous, mindful of both his human and his vampire needs. He thought it was probably the baby that was making them both more human, more aware of the limited time they might spend on the earth together. He laid awake at night while Del slept and wondered what the baby would be like. He wondered if it would be a boy or a girl, and almost shook Del awake to ask her if she would go for one of those tests to find out the baby's sex. But he withdrew his hand before he touched her shoulder. She couldn't go for tests like that, could she? Wouldn't the doctor wonder about her blood, wouldn't it be different or something? It was hard for him to believe that he and Del were really vampires, about to bring an innocent child into a world where society

207

refused to accept their kind.

When he tired of sitting in the neighborhood bar across from the boutique, Adragon sat in the Mustang. Since he left home early, he was usually lucky enough to get a parking space close enough to afford him a good view of Del's customers as they came and went.

After he had been on his stakeout for about a week, there was a day when he thought that his feet were turning to size eleven cubes of ice. He turned the heat on and off, warming up the car, then letting it cool down again. He made himself a mental note to ask Del why he couldn't just warm himself at will. Weren't vampires supposed to have magical powers or something?

He was parked across the street today, in front of the little bar that was beginning to feel like his home away from home. His eyes were fixed on the front door of the boutique, and he was beginning to feel foolish. He admitted to himself that it wasn't very likely that Del's attacker would show up at the shop in broad daylight and do something that would point to him as a suspect.

Adragon's eyes were heavy, and he must have dozed off for a few seconds. He didn't see anyone approach the car, and when there was a tap on the window a couple of inches from his face, he almost jumped through the roof.

A sudden sharp pain in his neck indicated that his head had been slumped forward at an unnatural angle. He rubbed the back of his head as he turned quickly to peer out the window, expecting to see a cop asking for his ID.

Instead, he looked directly into the inquisitive

brown eyes of his mother's neighbor, Raymond Sadler. Raymond was bent over, so that his face was on the same level as Adragon's, and he was smiling. Adragon's first reaction was one of annoyance, but it quickly changed to gratitude for the sight of a familiar face.

"Ray!" Adragon hit the button that lowered the window and a cold draft of air flowed into the car. "How are you doing, man?"

"I'm fine, Adragon, absolutely fine, and you?"

"I'm great, Ray."

"You look tired, my boy. Are you monitoring your sugar every day, taking your insulin?"

"Sure." Adragon smiled, wondering what Raymond would say if he just blurted out that he was a vampire now, way beyond such mundane things as glucose levels and insulin dosages.

"How's Mom?" he asked to change the subject. He remembered very clearly the time Raymond had checked his blood sugar level in the restaurant parking lot, and he definitely didn't want a repeat of that performance today.

"Physically, Elsbeth is fine. Emotionally, she's not at her best. You must know that she's not too pleased with your actions."

"I don't want to talk about that, Ray, okay?"

"I understand, and I certainly respect your wishes."

"Thanks, Ray. What uh—what are you doing in Point Pleasant anyway?"

"A little post-holiday shopping, my boy, but I'm not having much luck finding what I'm looking for. Maybe you and I should investigate that new restaurant they've been advertising on TV,

209

Sir-something-or-others?"

"Ray, you have some really great ideas. I'm up for it if you are."

Later, after a good healthy seafood lunch and another lecture about watching his sugar level, Adragon drove slowly home, ready for an afternoon nap. He was stretched out on Del's bed, drifting toward sleep, when it crossed his mind that Raymond hadn't asked him what *he* was doing dozing in a car in Point Pleasant on a cold January morning. "Peculiar," he mumbled to himself, before he came to the realization that Elsbeth had put him up to it. They had probably called the condo first, and since he wasn't there, Elsbeth had assumed that he would be at the boutique with Del. She must have sent Raymond there to intercept him and invite him out to lunch. He wanted to be angry, but he couldn't, because he knew that she was just looking out for him, just worrying about his health. "You're a piece of work, Elsbeth," he mumbled to himself just before he dropped off to sleep.

When Del's alarm went off the next morning, Adragon turned over and buried his head under his pillow. The next time he woke up, it was after eleven, and he knew that his days of trailing Del to and from work were over.

Chapter Twenty-one

The next two weeks passed uneventfully, at least for a young man going through the metamorphosis Adragon was experiencing. He had nearly put Del's beating behind him when she told him that she had to attend a special meeting of the Society of Vampires the following night.

His immediate reaction was to grab her shoulders and shake her until her teeth rattled.

"You're so damned stubborn," he told her. "You know who you need to be protected from? From yourself, that's who."

But when he saw that there was no moving her from the accomplishment of her goal, Adragon relented.

"Okay, you're right, of course, you have to go," he said, and she bought his act completely.

"Thank you for understanding, sweet Adragon," she murmured, and kissed away what she thought to be his last doubts. Actually, he had abandoned the idea of throttling her in favor of a new plan. He intended to follow her to the important Society meeting, find out its secret location, and spy on its members at the same time he was protecting Del.

Once it was settled that she would go, Adragon

started reliving the terrible night he had found her in her bed, gray and close to death. He remembered how she had been roughed up by a member of the Society, either by its leader or with his (her?) consent. He renewed his vow to learn the identity of his lover's attackers, and to punish them for what they had done to her.

The next morning Adragon was still wondering how he could arrange to follow Del when he had no idea what time of night the meeting would be held, when fate stepped in. He was taking a shower when the phone rang, and he hurried out of the bathroom assuming that Del had already left the condo. He put the receiver to his ear, opened his mouth to say "hello," and heard Del's voice.

He was already lowering the phone when her caller spoke, and he felt a jolt of recognition. He had to bite his lip to keep from blurting her name out loud. His mother was calling his lover, and it didn't sound as if he was the subject of their conversation.

"I am but the messenger, Delphine," Elsbeth said coldly.

"Why didn't he call me himself? Is he afraid that I'll refuse?"

"Hardly." There was a hard tone of mockery in Elsbeth's voice that Adragon recognized from his many arguments with her over the years.

"He wants you to prepare for the meeting, and you have no right to question his orders," Elsbeth reminded Del.

Who, damn it, who is he? Say his name, Adragon begged silently, *say his name.*

"What about my business?" Del insisted. "This is

212

awfully short notice, what am I supposed to do about the shop?"

"That really isn't my problem, is it?" Elsbeth asked sweetly.

"I'll have to close early, by around three o'clock, and I don't have anyone to come in on Thursdays. He hasn't forgiven me." Del sounded desolate, and Adragon wanted to say something to comfort her. "That's it, isn't it?"

"Oh, don't be so damned melodramatic. It's just another one of his games."

"Is it?" Del wondered. "I'm not so sure."

"Just be there," Elsbeth advised, "you wouldn't want to disappoint him again." She hung up then, and Adragon waited until Del broke the connection before he replaced the receiver and walked naked into the living room, drying his hair with the red bath sheet.

"Who was on the phone?" he asked, trying to sound casual.

"One of my part-time girls from work," Del answered. She was assembling her purse and keys and stuffing something into a canvas bag, and she didn't look up when Adragon entered the room.

"Anything wrong?"

"A minor problem with a customer. Nothing I can't handle."

"It must be nice, being the big boss lady."

"What?" Del asked distractedly. "Oh, believe me, it's not what it's cracked up to be."

As soon as she left the apartment, Adragon started to make plans. He knew that he would have to be careful so that Del wouldn't be blamed for alerting him to the day or time of the meeting. According to what he had learned from both Del and Elsbeth, all members of the Society of Vampires were sworn to secrecy, and would be punished if they broke their silence about Society rules or disclosed information to nonmembers. He knew that Del had only told him about the meeting because he would panic if she turned up missing from the apartment late at night.

Adragon thumbed through the telephone directory until he found a car rental agency that specialized in old, cheap, nondescript automobiles. He dialed their number, gave them his name, and arranged to have their oldest, most unidentifiable vehicle delivered to him in the parking lot of a popular restaurant in Toms River in two hours. If the person who dealt with him thought that was a strange request, he didn't say so.

"Money talks," Adragon said to himself when he hung up the phone. As an incentive for their discretion, he had offered to pay the agency a month's rental fee in advance, in cash, at the time they delivered the car to him.

He arrived at the rendezvous site early, parked his Mustang in the center of a group of early lunch patrons' vehicles, and hung out near the entrance, as though he was waiting for a luncheon date, until the car arrived right on time. At first glance, it was much better looking than Adragon would have liked, but he took it anyway, since he really didn't have a choice. It was a four-year-old mid-size Chevy, which could have been black, blue, or green, depending on the light. He decided that it was a good choice, and that the rental agency had probably dealt with customers like him before.

After he was sure that the guy who delivered the car was gone, Adragon drove the Mustang down the street and left it on the outer fringes of the huge parking lot of a discount department store. Even if it was there after closing time, he doubted very much if it would be bothered, or checked out by the local cops. Then he walked back to the restaurant, went inside, ordered a burger and a Coke, ate, returned to the Chevy and drove away, all without attracting any undue attention.

He made a quick trip back to the condo, changed into jeans and a black turtleneck sweater under his brown leather jacket, then drove to Del's boutique. It was almost two-thirty when he arrived there, and he hoped that he wouldn't have too long to wait.

He almost missed Del when she left the shop forty-five minutes later. She was wearing jeans and a denim jacket, instead of the red suit she had been wearing when she left for work in the morning. He wondered if that's what she'd been stuffing in the tote bag, or if she kept an extra set of clothes at the boutique for just such emergencies. But while he didn't recognize her clothes, he couldn't have missed her glorious hair which lay like a golden mantle on her shoulders.

When Del pulled her red Nissan out of the small parking lot behind the store and entered the flow of southbound traffic, he followed several car lengths behind in the nondescript Chevy. Traffic was fairly heavy, so he had no trouble keeping her car in sight without exposing himself.

He followed the red car through Bayhead and several other little shore towns, on through Mantoloking, into the outskirts of Seaside Heights, where Del turned away from the water and headed west into Toms River. She drove straight down Route 37, and Adragon had a bad minute when he thought she was onto him. But she passed the lot where the Mustang was parked without a glance in its direction and continued driving until she came to a cutoff that took them south into a sparsely populated area of town.

Soon there were no other cars on the street with them, and Adragon was forced to drop back out of Del's sight. She weaved in and out of narrow, unpaved streets that were home to small construction companies and warehouses, a lot of which appeared to be abandoned.

He thought he had actually lost Del when he lost sight of her, then came to a cross street and had to guess which way she might have turned. He decided to turn right, because there wasn't much in that direction, except a couple of small buildings that had definitely seen better days. When he turned his head to the left to make sure the road he was turning into was free of traffic, he caught a flash of red, and hastily turned the wheel to the left.

He drove down the road toward the area where he thought he had seen the Nissan, and although he couldn't spot it from the street, he was fairly sure it had disappeared behind one of a group of aluminum-sided buildings several hundred feet down the street. The area looked to Adragon as if it had been designed to be the site of an industrial park for small to mid-size businesses. One reason he thought Del had stopped there, was that there simply wasn't anyplace else she could have disappeared so quickly.

He drove the Chevy past the line of buildings,

216

seven or eight of them in all, and parked out of sight behind a stand of trees that acted as a buffer between them and a rather decrepit residential area that backed up to them. Then he walked back, examined each of the buildings, and ascertained that they were all unoccupied.

Del's Nissan was parked behind the third building down from where Adragon was parked. Since the car was empty, he assumed that she was inside, making the preparations she had discussed with Elsbeth on the phone. When he heard the door of the building creak, Adragon jumped out of sight around the corner and watched as Del came out, opened the trunk of her car, began removing cardboard boxes and carrying them inside the building.

When she had all of the boxes inside the building, she closed the door and remained inside. Adragon waited two or three minutes, then crept up to the door he had seen Del enter and tried the knob. He wasn't surprised to find that she had locked it behind her. After all, it was almost dark now, and this wasn't the best part of town.

He walked completely around the building, but there were no other doors, and the windows were sealed shut. There seemed to be no other course for him to take but to return to the Chevy and wait.

Del was inside the building for an hour and a half. When she emerged, carrying the empty cardboard boxes, the sky was black and the evening air was cold. After she drove away, Adragon made one more circuit of the building on foot before climbing into the rental car and driving back to the downtown area. He stopped at a 7-Eleven, and bought two large containers of black coffee and a ham and

217

cheese sandwich. He left them in the car while he dialed Del's number from a pay phone around the side of the building.

"Hello," she answered after several rings, sounding tired to Adragon. Of course, he was hoping that she was tired, maybe too exhausted to make the meeting she had just prepared for.

"Hi, it's me."

"Adragon, where are you?"

"I'm in Asbury," he lied, "with Jeff—you remember, the guy from my psych class?"

"Yes, I remember your mentioning him," Del said, although Adragon was sure he had never mentioned Jeff to her.

"Yeah. Well, he has this new bike, a Harley, and he wants me to check it out. Since you're going out tonight, I thought what the hell, I may as well have some fun, too. Unless you want me to come home for something."

"No," Del answered too quickly. "By all means stay and enjoy yourself with uh—"

"Jeff."

"Yes, Jeff."

"I guess I'll see you later tonight, huh?"

"Yes, of course. I may be late."

"I'll wait up for you."

"That won't be necessary. Just enjoy yourself with your friend."

"You, too."

He was replacing the receiver when she spoke again, and he moved it back to his ear quickly.

"Adragon?"

"Yeah, I'm here."

"I love you."

"I love you, too, Del. And the baby. Take care of the baby, okay?"

She didn't answer, and Adragon was glad that he had followed her, in spite of the fact that he felt guilty about lying to her. She had sworn to him that her punishment was complete. "It's over," she had said repeatedly. But was it really over? If it was, why did she sound so damned dismal?

He sat in the Chevy and finished the first container of coffee, and thought about what he was about to do. He hadn't prayed for a long time, and he wasn't sure that vampires' prayers were answered, but he said one anyway. Then he drove the dark, ordinary-looking car past the building where he had followed Del earlier, into the residential area beyond it.

He parked at the end of a street where several of the houses looked dark, as if maybe their occupants hadn't yet returned from their jobs for the evening. Hopefully, each of them would think that the car belonged to someone else on the street. He walked back toward the abandoned industrial park site, slowly, with his head down, his hands in his pockets, trying his best to look as inconspicuous as the car he had left at the end of the street. The only thing a nosey neighbor might have found suspicious was the fact that he carried a picnic lunch, a 7-Eleven bag containing a big ham and cheese sandwich and a container of hot coffee.

It was amazingly simple to pick the lock on the door behind which lay the trappings of the Society of Vampires. Adragon marveled at their lack of security, after all their lies and secrets. Once inside, he waited tensely for several minutes, half-expecting the wail of sirens to signal the fact that he had tripped a silent alarm. When several minutes passed without someone pounding on the door and yelling "Police," he relaxed and started looking around the interior of the building.

It was bigger than it looked from the outside. There was a main room, which was furnished with a long wooden table, twelve or fourteen chairs, a fireplace, and several smaller pieces of furniture, which Adragon figured were probably used to hold serving dishes for their banquets or props for their ceremonies. There were two adjoining rooms, both smaller than the main room, one of which was a kitchen of sorts, with a sink and an apartment-size range which wouldn't be much good for cooking for a dozen people.

The third room was the one which interested Adragon. It was small, maybe eight feet square, and completely empty. The tile floor sloped down from the sides to a large drain in the middle. The walls were covered with the same spotless white tile as the floor. There wasn't anything threatening about the room, but it was somehow obscene. The entire room sparkled, and Adragon thought that maybe that had been one of Del's chores, to prepare the room for tonight's ceremonies. It must have been, because other than that, there was no sign that she had been there, and no evidence of the contents of the cardboard boxes she had carted into the building, except for some cleaning supplies and several freshly laundered black robes. Adragon felt a stirring in the pit of his stomach; he was getting a bad feeling that he should never have let Del come here, to this room which he seriously wished he had never seen.

Somewhere deep in his subconscious mind, a half-formed memory vied for Adragon's attention, but he didn't allow it to surface. If he had a memory of this room, or of some other room like it, he didn't want to know about it. Fighting off the desire to bolt and run away from this place and the bad vibes it was throwing off, Adragon went back to the main room and started to search for a hiding place.

Chapter Twenty-two

Adragon had begun to think that his plan wouldn't work because there was obviously no place to hide. He scraped his foot across the floor in the main room, on the off chance that the Society had taken the time to dig a cellar under the building. They hadn't. Then he ran his hands over the walls, up and down, then across the expensive paneling they had used to bring the room up to their standards.

At first he thought it was his imagination; then with mounting excitement, he realized that he had found something. One narrow section of the paneling seemed to be recessed slightly between the two sections that bounded it on either side. He looked more closely at the floor, and saw that there was a dark mark on the floorboards beneath that section, as if something heavy had been dragged over them.

For what seemed like a long time, Adragon pushed and pounded on the section of the wall that didn't quite fit in with the others. He searched for some small abnormality, a bump or a hole hiding a secret switch that would move the door in or out. Finally, through sheer persistence, he found it, and it was so simple. When he laid his hand flat on the wall just to the left of the crooked little panel, he felt it vibrate, then start to move. It didn't swing in dramatically, like secret panels do in the movies. It moved sideways slowly, almost imperceptibly at first, until there was an opening in the wall eight or ten inches wide.

Adragon turned sideways and squeezed his body through the opening. The space beyond was coal black, and smelled as if it had been deprived of fresh air for a very long time. He felt around on the wall but there didn't seem to be a light switch of any kind. Putting one foot in front of the other, he edged across the wooden floor, wondering how soon he would slam into another wall.

Almost immediately, he encountered an object that clattered loud enough to wake the dead. A bucket, he reasoned, as the noise reverberated in his head.

Adragon made his way across the floor without further incident. As his eyes adjusted to the dark, he saw that he was in a tiny room, with a narrow recess in the side wall, which he had finally reached. He thought that he could probably hide in the recess without being seen, as long as there was no light in the room. Even if they opened the trick door, they wouldn't notice him unless they were looking for him. Of course, there was the problem of getting out of that tiny, airless room after the ceremony was over, but he knew that he couldn't let a minor problem like that stop him now.

Before he decided to close himself in the room, it was necessary to make absolutely sure that there was no light switch on the wall, no light cord dangling from the ceiling. A surprise like that could be disastrous. He took a precious half hour to search the dark room, before he could say without a doubt that there was no electrical switch or cord on his side of the sliding panel.

Then he lay down on the floor, put his rolled up leather jacket under his head, and rested, checking his watch every few minutes, until it finally read seven-thirty. He stood, stretched, peed in the small kitchen sink (where the hell was the toilet, behind another secret panel?) and splashed cold water on his face.

Adragon left the sliding panel slightly ajar, and waited in the dark recess on the far wall. He just stood there for a long time, and waited for the fun to begin.

The walls of the building were thick, and sounds from outside didn't penetrate to the recess where Adragon stood as still as a statue. The first thing he heard was the rattle of a key in the lock, and then the low murmur of voices as several people entered the building. When they filed into the main room, he almost peed his pants, he was so scared that one of them would approach his hiding place with a flashlight, or flip the switch that he hadn't been able to locate, and flood the black room with light.

At first, Adragon had trouble sorting out the individual voices. Eventually though, he recognized Del and Elsbeth and several people he had met at the one Society meeting he had attended, the young guy who had gone to the condo with the donors, and the older woman with the wattled neck, among others.

They chatted quietly among themselves, but Adragon sensed an air of expectancy. He heard chairs being moved around, and it sounded as if a slight disagreement ensued between two of the women whose voices he couldn't place. His stomach growled when he picked up the smell of fresh bread and strong cheese, although he had finished off the ham and cheese sandwich and stuffed the telltale wrappings in his jacket pocket. A cork popped and he heard another noise that could have been wine splashing into glasses.

Adragon began to share the members' sense of anticipation. Something was about to happen, and he was sure it had little to do with the food or wine that was being set out on the banquet table. They were all waiting anxiously for something and Adragon waited with them.

About an hour after the first members had arrived, just when Adragon was beginning to wonder how long he could stand to remain in his hiding place without giving himself away, the group fell silent. Adragon closed his eyes and tried to imagine what they were doing in the banquet room, as the outside door opened and a blast of cold air traveled into the corner where he waited.

The person who now entered the building had to be the group's leader, the man who had caused Del to be beaten half to death. Adragon knew that, and it was hard to keep his silence. He wanted desperately to jump from the dark room and stand in the light, face to face with the man he hated without knowing his name. He swore to himself that he would know the man's identity before the evening ended.

Adragon strained to hear the man's voice, but the outer room had fallen strangely silent, and the deadly quiet was unnerving. Besides that, his legs were beginning to cramp from standing in his little hole in the wall, and Adragon was tempted to step out into the room and stretch his legs. It was a good thing that he didn't, because only a second later, the door to the inner room slid open. Adragon stiffened, and prepared to defend himself, sure that he would be discovered and dragged out into the light.

Instead, something was tossed into the room, something heavy by the sound it made hitting the floor. The parties who had thrown it left quickly and as they moved away from the doorway, light from the outer room seeped in. Adragon was shocked to discover that the "something" that now occupied the room with him was a boy of fifteen or sixteen, bound and gagged, his dark eyes huge with fright.

When the boy saw Adragon, his eyes bugged out even further and, if he hadn't been gagged, Adragon was sure the boy would have cried out. He tried to slide across the floor, to get further away from Adragon, but he was unable to move more than a few inches. His face and arms were covered with red splotches, turning to black and blue. He had obviously been beaten, maybe by the same person who had beaten Del.

Adragon didn't know what to do. If they intended to let the kid go, why had they thrown him in this dark room while they carried on their ceremony? Maybe they didn't intend to release him. Maybe he was to be a part of their ritual.

Adragon shook his head and smiled, chastising himself for letting his imagination run away with him. He had almost decided to step out of his hiding space and stand up for the boy, insist that he be untied and released, when another boy entered the room and knelt beside the captive. Adragon recognized the boy who had just entered as the kid who had come home with Del the night the donors were there. What was his name, Weldon, or something like that?

"I'm sorry, Robbie, honest to God I am. I haven't been in the Society that long. I didn't know what they'd do to you," the newcomer whispered to the boy on the floor. "They asked me if I had a friend, like they were going to invite you to join or something. I thought it would be fun. I wish there was something I could do, but there isn't."

Weldon (if that was his name) reached to push the boy's straight dark hair off his forehead, but the boy shook his head and turned away from his one-time friend.

"Hey, Robbie, we've been good friends. Don't die hating me, okay?" Weldon begged, with tears in his eyes. At the word "die," the boy on the floor became hysterical, screaming silently behind his gag, his eyes almost popping out of his head with fright.

Weldon left the room and returned two or three minutes later with a hypodermic needle which he inserted into the other boy's arm and pushed the plunger. Adragon noticed that Weldon didn't bother with an alcohol swab—no sense in worrying about sterile conditions when the kid was going to die soon anyway.

After Weldon left the room a second time, the silence in the other room was broken, and Adragon's uneasiness grew in proportion to the level of noise. The Society members were chanting, moving around, dancing maybe, and Adragon wondered if any of them were really sane, even the ones he loved. He thought it was strange that he hadn't heard the voice of their leader yet, and he was growing impatient to learn the man's identity. Still, after Weldon's statement that his friend was slated to die, Adragon thought he'd probably better stay put and try to take the group by sur-

227

prise later, if the opportunity presented itself.

It could only have been fifteen or twenty minutes later when two robed figures entered the inner room, almost catching Adragon by surprise. He had been resting his head on the wall behind him, bending his knees to ease the tension he was feeling. He seriously thought that standing still for so long was harder on him now that he was a vampire than it would have been when he was entirely human. He was strung so tight now, so tense all the time, that he always felt as if he might burst out of his skin at any given moment.

One of the hooded figures turned, and Adragon recognized Del by the shimmer of her red hair, as it caught the light that filtered in from the other room. The second figure was larger, probably a man. They knelt and bent over the boy, who hadn't moved since Weldon had injected him. Another person entered the room, and several others gathered around the door. Adragon stood as still as he could, scared to death that he would move and alert the Society to his presence. The air in the room suddenly seemed very close, and he tried not to breathe, afraid that he would sneeze or cough or inhale loud enough to call attention to himself.

Then his fears were forgotten as the men and women in the room with him started to chant, followed by the others. Their voices were high and shrill, on the edge of hysteria, and they rose from a low murmur to a loud cacophony that filled every corner of the building. Adragon's imagination was working overtime on what they were going to do to the unconscious boy, and all of the ideas he came up with were bad ones.

As several more people pushed their way into the

inner room, Adragon tried to sink deeper into the recess that hid him from their sight. There was a smell in the air, the odor of incense, and he was beginning to feel light-headed. He closed his eyes for a second, and when he opened them, a tall figure clad in red towered over him. Adragon raised his eyes and looked into the eyes of the leader of the Society of Vampires, into the eyes of Raymond Sadler.

Chapter Twenty-three

The leader spoke, and it was his voice, familiar and known, that drove Adragon over the edge. He jumped at the man with the intention of knocking him to the ground, but hands reached out for him, and he was stopped before he could so much as touch Raymond Sadler.

"Adragon, you stupid fool, why did you come here, why didn't you stay at home where you belong?"

"You bastard!" Adragon growled. His head was spinning, his heart racing at a wild, uncontrollable speed. He could barely comprehend that this man he had thought to be a friend could be the same inhuman creature who had beaten Del so badly. He lowered his head and tried again to dive at Raymond, to butt him in the chest. This time, he felt something strike him on the back of the head as he moved away from the wall, and he sank down into a well of darkness.

For hours that dragged into unmeasurable units of time, Adragon floated in the black confines of his own mind, below the level of conscious thought. Strange, surreal images drifted in and out of his brain, frightening, mind-bending pictures of a horrible ceremony and the screams of a young boy.

Adragon awoke trembling with fear, nearly blind from the pain that pounded in his head and reverberated through his body. He opened his eyes to slits, and saw only darkness. He tried to move, and thought for a horrible moment that he was paralyzed, before realizing that his hands and feet were bound. The floor beneath him was rough and cold, and he figured he was probably in the same room where he had been discovered by the Society members and their leader. He could see his feet stretched out in front of him, tied at the ankles with heavy rope.

Suddenly, he remembered the boy who had been held captive in this room, and the awful screams that had seeped into his unconscious mind after he had been knocked out. He felt nauseous, and the ham and cheese sandwich threatened to come up. He saw in his mind, very clearly, as if he had been there, a ceremony where a young man's heart was cut out of his chest with a long, sharp blade. He then thought about the tile room with the drain in the center, and he knew exactly what it was used for. The ham and cheese bit into his stomach, and he leaned over to vomit onto the floor. When he raised his head again, someone spoke his name, and he realized that he wasn't alone.

Adragon forced his eyes open wider, even though it caused him excruciating pain to do so. What he thought he saw in the dark room caused him to blink several times, to clear his vision. He forgot his pain for a minute, and struggled unsuccessfully to work his hands free of the rope that bound him. He didn't want to believe his eyes, but he knew that the scene that unfolded in front of him was real. To his right, several feet away from him, the two women he loved most in the world were shackled hand and foot to a pole that appeared to be the major support of the ceiling above them.

"Elsbeth? Del? Where are we?"

"We're in Raymond's basement," Del answered calmly, even as Elsbeth's voice rose hysterically, calling out her son's name.

"What are we doing here?" Adragon asked, hoping that Del wouldn't lose her cool until he had some sense of exactly what was happening.

"He's going to kill us, he's going to kill all three of us," Elsbeth moaned, and Adragon saw confirmation of that terrible fact in Del's eyes.

His head was still pounding, and Adragon had a hard time concentrating. He also had a hard time taking the situation seriously. Raymond loved Elsbeth; why in the world would he suddenly decide that he wanted to kill her? He repressed a nervous giggle and shook his head to clear it of the cobwebs. His first clear thought was that Del and Elsbeth were both scared, so this situation must be real, and it must be serious.

"Where are you, Raymond?" Adragon asked in a loud, steady voice that echoed through the cavernous cellar. The silence of the great house above him was his only answer.

"Raymond!" Adragon's voice boomed, witness to his returning strength and the knowledge that he was more than human, vampire dealing with vampire.

"Show yourself, you lousy chicken-shit bastard!" he challenged, and he was rewarded by a movement in the shadows at one corner of the room.

"No need to get nasty, Adragon," Raymond answered from the spot where he had waited for his adversary to regain consciousness.

"You son of a bitch, untie me, and I'll show you nasty."

"Calling me names won't help your situation, my boy."

The aging vampire leader stepped from the shadows, and Adragon felt a flash of fear. The loose jogging suits and suit jackets usually worn by the man had completely hidden the extent of his excellent physical condition. Raymond had the body of a twenty-year-old, and it was shown to advantage in red tights and a form-fitting red shirt that disclosed every inch of his well-honed body.

"You'd better have one hell of a good reason for doing this, Ray," Adragon blustered, "because when I get out of here—"

"You would have done well to remember some of the lessons learned at your sainted mother's knee," Raymond said as he moved forward, eyes flashing dangerously. He moved rapidly toward Adragon, and his aggressive behavior frightened the younger man. Adragon lost his train of thought and shrank away as the leader approached him. Elsbeth mumbled something unintelligible, and Raymond turned his head, to silence her with his eyes, before he turned his attention back to her son.

"I'm in charge here, Adragon. In case you haven't noticed, I have detained both your mother and your lover against their will. I think you will be forced to cooperate with me, to ensure their safety, as well as your own."

"But why are you doing this, Ray? I thought we were friends."

"Friends? *Friends?*" The old vampire's laughter echoed in the huge, empty basement, before he turned deadly serious. "You have displeased me, Adragon Hart. You have delved into things that do

233

not concern you. You have forced me to take action against you."

"I'm sorry, Ray, honest to God I am." Adragon's answer was almost sincere. He knew that he was in no position to further antagonize the man, and he was damned sorry to be so completely helpless.

"Don't patronize me, Adragon, it's too late for your inane apologies. The laws of the Society of Vampires have been violated, you have trespassed into our sanctuary and witnessed our ancient ceremonies. You are surely not fool enough to think that there will be no punishment for these acts."

"For Christ's sake, Ray, this is turning into a scene from a B movie. I said I was sorry."

Raymond turned his back on Adragon and walked toward the spot where Elsbeth and Del sat on the cold floor, their hands and feet chained to the center pole. Adragon tried to think fast, despite his continued headache, to come up with something that might distract Raymond's attention for a little longer, until he could think of some way to make him release the women.

The vampire leader spun suddenly, and fixed his cold eyes on Adragon's face.

"Whatever clever idea you may conceive, you would best abandon it. As leader of the Society, I have a sacred duty to uphold, and your life is not sacred to me unless it is sacred to the Society. I have killed, and I will kill again, to preserve our integrity. I could wring your neck without the least hesitation, although I have long admired you from afar, and would have taken you with me now, had I thought you were the least inclined to follow me."

As Raymond raved on, a picture of the girl from Asbury Park, the girl whose body had washed up on the beach near Raymond's house, swam into view before Adragon's eyes.

"What about the girl, Ray? Did you kill the girl?"

Adragon had thought the man would try to deny it, but he didn't. "Of course, I killed her, the silly little tramp. She was dangerous. She was confiding to her friends about the handsome young man who mesmerized her into being his willing victim."

"No one would have believed her."

"Wishful thinking on your part. You put our entire group in jeopardy, Adragon. I couldn't allow it."

"You're a crazy old man."

"No," Ray shook his head and smiled sadly. "Not crazy, but old, yes, old in human terms. I'm afraid I've overstayed my welcome on the earth, my boy. It's time I rested and chose a new life. I wish you would go with me, but I wouldn't take you against your will. If I'd wanted to do that, I could have taken you long ago."

Adragon was still trying to make some sense out of Ray's words when Elsbeth spoke up. "Raymond is still in his first incarnation, Adragon."

"I don't understand. What does that mean?"

"It means that he has lived in the same smelly old body for hundreds of years, changing his name and his location when his neighbors began to get suspicious, but never allowing himself to stop his heart and join us in the other place."

Adragon looked at the older man with new respect, although he could hardly fathom the idea that he was looking at an ancient vampire, one who had lived for hundreds of years.

Chapter Twenty-four

"I have led a strange and wonderful life," Raymond expostulated, walking back and forth in front of his prisoners as if he were an actor on a stage, "one long, long lifetime filled to overflowing with an excess of both joy and pain.

"But you . . . you, my boy, were raised as a mortal, unaware of your specialness. Your life has been extraordinary. You have had Elsbeth for a partner, a guide, but she chose not to enlighten you. Do you realize that had it not been for the Society, you might not have become aware of your background in this lifetime?"

Raymond seemed to be waiting for an answer, and Adragon told him that yes, he did realize that he owed something to the Society.

"She didn't know how to tell you," Raymond went on, "but I had known Elsbeth's secret for years. I even tested your unbelievably sweet blood for her, she was so fearful of your human frailty. Many times I begged her to let you taste blood, so that your disease would no longer be a threat to your life. But she was, as always, fearful. Of what, Elsbeth?

"Never mind, we will get to that later," he ordered when Elsbeth hesitated. "We have little time left, and there is still much to be said."

"Little time?" Adragon asked, trying to stall, wondering what to do next. Listening to Raymond seemed to be getting him nowhere. He had to come up with a way to convince the man to free Del and Elsbeth, even if he had to offer himself in their place.

"I must admit that I was often tempted to feed you myself," Raymond was saying when Adragon tuned in again, "to awaken that strong, young body to all the sensual pleasures of vampirism. But I digress. We have roughly—" Raymond glanced at a thin gold watch on his wrist, tapped it with his index finger, and smiled at Adragon. "Roughly two hours and ten minutes."

"Until what?" Adragon asked.

"Until this place blows sky high, dear boy. Oh, don't fret, I have no intention of blowing you up with it, my feelings for you still run too deep for that. Unless, of course, you can't choose. In that case, you may very well perish, in one hundred and twenty minutes, more or less."

"Unless I choose?" Adragon's adrenaline was flowing, and he was straining against the ropes that held him immobile.

Raymond raised his arm in a wide, sweeping gesture that included Elsbeth and Del, both of whom were watching him with intense interest.

"If you wish to live, you must choose which one of your lovers will live on with you . . . and which one will die with me."

"You're crazy."

Ray threw back his head and laughed good-naturedly. "Dear boy, you should never tell a man who has you hog-tied in a basement with a bomb set to go off that he's crazy. You are quite amusing, but you are becoming repetitive, my boy, and I'm afraid we have no time for such an indulgence."

"Ray, you wouldn't make me do that, would you, make me choose?"

"Oh, yes, I quite definitely would do that. As a matter of fact, I hope you're already pondering your decision, since your time is fast running out."

"How can I choose, Ray? You can't expect me to choose either one of them over the other. Elsbeth's my mother, for Christ's sake."

"And Del is your lover."

"Well, yeah, but—"

"Decide," Raymond said simply, and Adragon knew that he might have to do just that.

"Before I choose, Ray, what happened to that boy tonight? Did you kill him, too?"

"You were there, Adragon, don't you remember?"

"No, I don't."

"The boy is dead. Who killed him is of little consequence. Now I really must insist that you stop wasting time and get on with arriving at your decision."

"One more question, Ray, you owe me that."

"Quickly then, before I change my mind."

"Why did you beat Del? Was it because she's pregnant?"

Adragon heard his mother gasp, and out of the corner of his eye, he saw her hand fly to her mouth to stifle a cry, but he couldn't look her in the eye, because he knew how disappointed in him she must be at this moment.

"I'm surprised you have to ask such a question,

238

Adragon. She wasn't supposed to seduce you, that wasn't part of my master plan. Elsbeth was to join the Society, to write a book about us. By the way, if you do not choose to save your mother's mortal life, the book is in her office, nearly finished. Perhaps you will publish it under your own name and chart your own course to fame and fortune.

"Be that as it may, you were to be mine, my boy, to belong to the leader of the great Society of Vampires. Does that really surprise you? But you were not to be forced. You were to be courted in the old tradition, which frequently linked man with man. That is why Del was beaten, for taking you away from her leader."

Adragon couldn't believe what he was hearing, but neither Del nor Elsbeth spoke up to deny Raymond's claims.

"Let him go, Raymond." The sound of Elsbeth's voice, forceful and clear, shocked both of the men.

Raymond smiled broadly and it was clear that Elsbeth was infuriated. "Let him go, damn it. What has he ever done to you?"

"For one thing, he has rejected me, refused to give me even a tiny scrap of his affection. I have killed for less than that, Elsbeth."

"He never did anything to you, why do you want to hurt him?" Del's voice was as soft and deep as velvet in the black room.

"Hurt Adragon? No, you clearly misunderstand my motives, Del. I want to hurt no one. I am old and tired, tired of my vampire life, and I am ready to make the transition to the waiting place, and another life. I was originally chosen to be your leader because of my strength, my cunning, my fearless nature. If the truth be known, I can no longer stand up to the outside forces that threaten to overcome us. It is time for me to rest."

"What I don't understand, Ray," Adragon interrupted, "is why you don't just go ahead and stop your heart. Why do you have to take somebody with you?"

"Because I am afraid, my boy. Strange admission for a vampire leader, that of fear. But yes, I admit that I am afraid of going to that place alone, that place where I have never before traveled. I need someone, someone I love, to stand beside me on the journey, to hold my hand, if you will."

"But why Del or Elsbeth? There must be someone else."

"There have been many, but they have all traveled on ahead of me."

"I still don't understand why you stayed so long in one incarnation," Adragon said, hoping to keep Raymond talking.

"You are a vampire who has lost his accumulation of knowledge, Adragon. I assume it will all come back to you in time, if you choose to stay on this earth. You probably don't remember that all vampires do not practice reincarnation. Many live in the guise of mortality for countless centuries, spending years sleeping in a box of dirt, preserving their youthful appearance, then awakening to find a new life and a new name. Each has his own reason for his choice.

"As for myself, I have always loved the earth, and never chosen to leave it, to spend time alone in the dark place, waiting to be reborn. I have had no desire to relinquish my power, to be a child again, barely capable of managing my own bodily functions."

240

"But that's what you're choosing now."

"I have explained quite patiently and thoroughly that I now require the complete rejuvenation that comes with rebirth. Enough life is enough, and I am old now, even for a vampire."

"But what if something goes wrong, like it did with me, and you aren't a vampire in the next life?" Adragon asked.

"I will always be a vampire, my boy, just as you were always a vampire, although your knowledge was hidden behind the veil of forgetfulness. I am sure both Del and Elsbeth are aware, even if you are not, that being a vampire is a greater torment than the human mind can fathom. It is also the greatest joy imaginable, a fulfillment a thousand times better than human sex.

"When a vampire makes love, he draws his lover to the threshold of eternity, to the fine edge, the line between mortal life and the dark place. If I were to awaken from my sleep as an ordinary human, stripped of my vampire nature, I fear that I might become a mass murderer or another Hitler. I am afraid that the very ordinariness of my life would overcome me."

"But, Ray," Adragon began before Raymond shook his head and glanced at his watch again. "No more stalling, Adragon. The three of you gathered in this room are the three vampire beings whom I love, that is the reason why you are here. Your time is fleeting, Adragon, and you seem no closer to a choice. Perhaps we should let your lovers plead their cases now."

"Ray, let's cut the crap, okay? Untie my mom and Del, and you and I can talk."

"Are you nobly offering yourself in return for my

hostages? A truly unselfish offer, and I wish I could accept you in their stead, Adragon, but I can not. Now I must ask you to hold your tongue while your mother speaks. Elsbeth . . ." Ray inclined his head in Elsbeth's direction. She took a deep breath before she looked into Adragon's eyes.

"I am your mother, Adragon," she said in a voice that quivered with fear. "All the years we've spent together must count for something." She started to cry and Adragon strained at his bonds, knowing that he would kill Raymond Sadler with his bare hands if he could free himself.

"Del?" Ray asked, "Can you top that?" The man seemed to be enjoying himself, and Adragon roared with anger.

"I love you, sweet Adragon," Del said calmly. "The decision is yours, not mine. We will be together again, in another life, because now that the link is forged, it will not be broken, not ever."

A few minutes ago, Adragon would have said that if he decided to take Ray seriously, he would have to choose Elsbeth. She was his mother, his companion through a hundred lifetimes. Now, he was moved by Del's kindness and her humility to want to stay with him for the rest of this lifetime and many more.

"How can I be expected to choose," he said aloud, "between two women that I love more than life itself?"

"Elsbeth," Raymond said, ignoring Adragon's remark, "I think it might be interesting to all of us if you told Adragon why the reincarnation chain was broken. I assume you haven't told him yet. Go on, tell him why you came back without him this time, and why you covered him with the veil of forgetfulness."

242

"Adragon doesn't care about that now," Elsbeth said, but the fact that her voice trembled when she said it was not lost on Adragon.

"Why don't you tell me about it, Mother?"

"No, please," Elsbeth moaned, and Adragon knew that he would have to hear it, in spite of the fact that they were using precious time.

"Go on," he insisted.

Raymond pulled a lawn chair close to the two women, sat down, and bent forward, listening eagerly.

Elsbeth shot him a look of pure hatred, then turned huge, misty eyes to Adragon. "Darling, you don't want to hear this."

"Talk, Mother, and no false starts, okay?"

She hesitated a moment more, still waiting for a reprieve from some corner. When none was forthcoming, she sighed and started to tell the story.

She was speaking aloud, in her human voice, but Adragon didn't hear her. She had taken control of his mind again, and pictures reeled off behind his eyes, a private theater of her thoughts.

There were two people on the screen, strangers to Adragon, slightly similar in appearance, except that one was a man and the other a woman. They were both remarkably beautiful, but the woman was breathtaking. Her long red hair was thick and lustrous, her body voluptuous, her skin the finest porcelain. Her brown eyes sparkled with reflected firelight and from the way she looked at the handsome man, it was clear that she adored him.

"Do you recognize them?" Elsbeth asked in a whisper. "Do you know who they are?"

"Yes. It's us, you and me."

"We were both so beautiful, so desirable, many

243

people of wealth and power begged for our favors."

Elsbeth's voice had taken on a faraway quality, as if she was reliving that long-ago lifetime.

Suddenly the stars of Adragon's private movie began to speak, and across the years, he heard his mother's voice.

"You must learn to trust me," the woman said, turning a sweet smile to the man.

"Don't be foolish, my love," he answered, "a woman as desirable as you can never be trusted."

"Are you accusing me of unfaithfulness?"

"You are flaunting it in my face, my love. If you persist in this behavior, I am afraid I shall be forced to lock you up . . . or something worse."

The man was smiling, but a cold chill ran down Adragon's spine. What did the man mean by "something worse?" Whatever he meant, was that the reason he and Elsbeth had been separated in this lifetime, for something that he had done to her out of jealousy?

"Enough." Raymond Sadler's voice cut into Adragon's dream of the past. "Preparations must be made. Sorry, my boy."

Adragon saw the blow coming but there was no way to avoid it with his hands tied behind his back. The wooden club caught him just above his left ear, and he went out like a light.

Chapter Twenty-five

The air in the basement was different when he came to again. He knew somehow that more than a few minutes had passed. Even though it was always dark in the basement, he sensed that it was getting on toward late afternoon. The floor felt damp under his legs, as if the tide had come in and seeped into the house, but he knew that wasn't it. The strong odor of gasoline filled his nostrils and made him want to gag. He moved his head to see how bad the blow with the wooden bat had been, and Raymond's voice came out of nowhere.

"Ah, Master Adragon has come back to us. I was beginning to think you might just sleep through all the festivities. It's time we got deadly serious, excuse the pun, about our reason for being here. Are you up to it, my boy?"

Adragon nodded, and lowered his aching head to his shoulder. He glanced down at his hands, and couldn't believe what he saw. His hands were free, as were his feet. Raymond must have untied him while he was unconscious. He tried to spring to his feet, but he fell back to the floor, weak and limp.

Finally, after several attempts, he was able to

stand, and to hobble toward the center pole where Del and Elsbeth were chained. To his surprise, Raymond now sat on the floor between them, his own hands and feet chained to the same center pole. He was holding a key in his hand, and he waved it in the air for Adragon's benefit, before folding his hand around it.

"You have only minutes left, Adragon, less than ten, and I hold the key to your future. You must either choose now, or I will have three escorts into my brief hereafter."

Seeing that key, which probably fit the locks on Del and Elsbeth's chains, and hearing Raymond's arrogant voice, Adragon went crazy. He lunged forward and dove at Raymond, striking the man a solid blow to the chest.

When Raymond fell backward against the pole, Elsbeth screamed and Del made a small sound in her throat that tore at Adragon's heart. If he could just get that key away from Raymond, he might have a chance to free the women and escape with them. If Raymond was telling the truth about the time frame, he had only a few minutes, and this would undoubtedly be his last chance to act.

He grabbed Raymond by the neck, intent on pounding the man's head against the pole until he lost consciousness, but he hadn't counted on the old vampire's extraordinary strength. Raymond threw his head back and roared, an ear-piercing inhuman howl, and bared incisors that looked as if they could rip a man's head off. He whipped his head back and forth so fast that it appeared to be a blur, all the time snapping at Adragon's hands with his fangs.

Adragon struggled to hold onto him without getting bitten, or struck a knockout blow by the man's head which was moving so fast that Adragon couldn't grab hold of it. His arms were aching badly from the strain of hanging onto the other man's neck, which seemed to have grown to gigantic proportions. The pain traveled up Adragon's arms and through his entire body, until he thought he would have to scream if it lasted one more second.

It was then that the center pole started to move, and ominous noises issued from the area of the ceiling above them. Bits of plaster dropped, Adragon could see it flying into Elsbeth's dark hair. More plaster fell, then a few splinters of wood, and Adragon realized that it would be too dangerous to continue shaking Raymond.

He dropped his hands from the man's neck and stepped away quickly, barely escaping Raymond's huge, sharp teeth. Now he feared that Raymond might use the key to free himself, and come after him. If he did, Adragon knew that he was no match for the old vampire's superior powers.

He also knew that the only way anyone of them could escape was for him to do what Raymond wanted and choose which woman he would sacrifice.

"Ray, if I still have a choice, I'm ready now," he said from a safe distance. The man's head movements had slowed down considerably, and he had stopped growling. Apparently, he was too agitated to think that he could use the key to his chains to enable him to chase Adragon down.

"You're a clever boy, Adragon," Raymond answered after several seconds, "but not quite as clever as you think. I could keep both of them, you know, since you have tried to cheat me out of a companion."

"You have your honor as a vampire leader, Ray. Anyway, I didn't try to distract you out of disrespect. You would have done the same thing, in my place."

"Yes . . . but we are out of time, Adragon. Your

choice must be swift if you are to escape with the chosen one."

"Del," Adragon said, and he could tell from the look on her face that she knew what he was going to say. "I love you, and I always will, but she's my mother."

Del nodded and looked down at her flat stomach, as if she could see the seed that grew there, the little girl or boy that would have someday belonged to them.

"I understand," she said finally, and Adragon reluctantly turned his attention to Elsbeth.

Raymond opened his fist and the small key rested in his palm. "Ah, Elsbeth," he said, "I shall miss you terribly."

Adragon expected some clever retort from his mother, but instead she kept her silence. She stared into his eyes, and all at once, he felt anxious to escape with her.

"Hurry," he urged her, but now she was looking at Del, at the same spot where Del's eyes rested, on the seed that would one day be her grandchild.

As he watched Elsbeth's face, a wave of nausea struck Adragon, and he felt as if he had been hit over the head again by the club Raymond had used on him. He wondered if he was suffering from a concussion, an injury that might prevent him from seeing his mother safely out of Raymond's huge old house before it blew up.

"Mother . . ." He clutched at his head and fought the images that took over his mind and rendered him helpless.

The two beautiful people, the man and the woman. She was surely more gorgeous than Elsbeth was in her current incarnation. Adragon watched as she licked her lips and teased the man who stood behind her, staring at her reflection as she applied lip-stick to her full, sensuous lips.

"Don't do that," the man ordered, but the woman ignored him and continued to meet his eyes in the mirror, mocking him with her laughter.

"I adore you, Charles," she said, and blew him a kiss on the tips of her white fingers.

"You adore everyone, you little whore, you adore the man you're seeing tonight. Well, I'm not going to let you go this time, Adrianna."

"And how will you stop me, brother?"

Brother! Adragon's mind reeled with the intricacies of the scene playing out before his eyes.

"I'll choke you if I have to," the man answered, and when the woman laughed again, he placed his hands on her beautiful throat.

"You couldn't," she challenged, and the man began to squeeze.

"Stop it, you're hurting me! Charles, stop! This isn't funny."

Adragon couldn't breathe. He bent over and clutched at his throat with trembling fingers. His eyes rolled back into his head, and he had almost lost consciousness before he realized that he had been the beautiful woman who died at her brother's hand, but that he did not have to die that way again.

"Let go of me," he yelled, and pushed away the in-visible presence that held him in its death grip. His windpipe opened up again, and he sucked in a great draft of air so fast that it almost tore his chest open.

Raymond was waiting, his eyes on Adragon's face, as if he knew exactly what was happening. The key was in his hand.

"Not her," Adragon said, indicating Elsbeth. Then he reached forward and took Del's hand, almost be-fore the chains slipped away and she was free.

"You must hurry, my boy," Raymond told him. "You have done the right thing. The child will be important to our future."

"Will you come back here, Ray?" Adragon asked as he dragged Del toward the steps that led to the first floor.

"I believe Elsbeth and I shall stay together now, Adragon, as you and Del shall stay together always. If she returns, you must look for me close by."

Having no reason to believe that Raymond was lying about the bomb, Adragon resisted the impulse to gather Del into his arms and hug her fiercely. Instead, he pulled her along, half-dragging her across the floor, toward their future.

"Come on," he urged her, "we've got to get the hell out of here."

"There is no time left," Raymond's voice boomed behind them, "you have failed to save her, Adragon." Then there was only his insane laughter, and the sound of Elsbeth's quiet weeping.

Adragon bolted up the stairs, pulling Del along behind him. As he ran, he was drawing a mental blueprint of the big house, trying to figure out which exit was nearer to the top of the stairs.

He didn't see the closed door at the top until he ran into it and Del ran into him from behind. His first thought was that Raymond had tricked them, that the door was locked. He prayed as he turned the knob and pushed. Nothing happened. He pulled, and the door creaked inward. Both he and Del had to step down so that he could open the door, and he was aware that he was using up precious seconds.

They found themselves in a room that held tall shelves of leather-bound books and a long comfortable-looking couch. After a moment's thought, Adragon ran across the room and through a door at

250

the far side, which led into a long empty hallway, with Del on his heels.

"Hurry, hurry," he panted, and Del squeezed his hand to indicate that she was trying. They were almost at the end of the hall when Adragon realized that he had made a bad mistake. He stopped abruptly and Del ran into him. He lifted her up and turned her around in the air, then sat her down facing the opposite way. With one hand around her waist, he half-carried her in the opposite direction from which they had just come.

In less than a minute, they were at the end of the hall, where he had to break a glass door that Raymond had locked, probably to delay them at the last minute.

Then they were outside, on the porch, racing down the steps that led to the beach. Del was lagging behind, pulling Adragon backward, and he stopped just long enough to lift her into his arms, marveling at how light she was. He ran with her across the sand toward the water, but the damp sand tugged at his feet and made it seem as if he was barely moving.

They were about two feet from the water's edge when the explosion came, and although he had been expecting it, Adragon couldn't believe that it had actually happened. He dove headfirst into the ocean, with Del still in his arms. She hit the water with a loud smack, and he dove in on top of her so that her body would be completely submerged, to protect her from the monstrous fire storm that was the result of Raymond's explosive charge and the gasoline that he had spread across the basement floor. Adragon stood quickly and reached down for Del, plucked her out of the sea, sputtering and coughing.

Until this moment, he hadn't had a chance to think about Elsbeth's totally unselfish act, because that's surely what it had been when she filled his mind with the final puzzle piece and admitted to him that she had murdered him in their last incarnation. So he had to assume that the reason she had left him behind in this lifetime was that she feared revenge. Or maybe she just couldn't face him with the truth. In any event, he wouldn't have believed that his mother was capable of such selfless behavior, and he wished that he had a chance to tell her how much he loved her one more time.

These thoughts ran through Adragon's mind as he pressed Del's body to his own and watched the bright orange and black cloud of flame and smoke rise above Raymond's house. He and Del stood in about a foot of water, several hundred feet from the house, but flaming debris rained down all around them. Del was shaking, and her eyes were wide with terror.

Adragon turned from his examination of her face and body and looked back at the house just in time to see a huge fireball rise upward to the heavens. He stared at the spot where the house had stood in amazement. There was nothing left, no walls, no windows, no roof, and only a few blocks of stone where the foundation had been. Nothing left of Raymond. Nothing left of Elsbeth, his mother, his companion, his friend.

Adragon threw back his head and screamed, a long, shrill cry of despair. "Mother!" he yelled, and the word burned his throat and threatened to sear his heart.

He pushed Del away from him and ran through the shallow water, back up the beach, toward the house. He wanted to sift through the little rubble that remained, searching for some sign of her. But Del's arms closed around him and she forced him to stop, not with her strength, but with her love. She threw herself against him, and wrapped her slim arms and legs around his body. She clung to him as if he was her lifeline, as she kissed his lips and gently stroked his scorched back with cool hands.

"Adragon, it's too late," she whispered, "there's nothing you can do now. She's gone. They're both gone."

He knew that she was right. He stood in the shallow water of his beloved ocean, as pieces of Ray's house floated around his legs.

"I'll miss her so much, I'm not sure I can make it without her," he sobbed.

"Are you sorry that you chose me?" Del asked him.

"No," he answered quickly, "I'll never be sorry about that."

But when Del knelt down in the water, he lifted his eyes heavenward and whispered, "I'm sorry, Elsbeth. Promise you'll come back to me soon. I'll never stop loving you."

He was shocked out of his reverie by the sound of Del's voice behind him. He turned to find her kneeling in the water, being battered back and forth by the waves churned up by the wind that was also fanning the fire.

"Pain," she murmured, tossing her head back and forth, "terrible pain."

Adragon reached her just as she slid sideways and fell into the water.

"Saving your life is beginning to be a habit," he told her minutes later, when the pain had passed and she was breathing easier.

"You'll have a lot of great stories to tell your daughter someday."

"Daughter? How do you know it won't be a boy."

"I know."

"Are you sure you're okay?" he asked, as they

started the long hike across the sand to Elsbeth's house, which stood untouched by its neighbor's destruction. Elsbeth's house, which was now his.

Del nodded and clung tighter to his arm as she walked along beside him.

"It was a soul, Adragon, a soul coming to claim our daughter. That's how it works, you know."

"No, I don't know."

"It's true. As soon as the pain struck, I knew what it was, although I've never experienced it before."

"You've never had a child before, not even in another life?"

"Never, until now."

"And this soul just popped out of the blue and settled into our little girl, and now she has a soul of her own? You really believe that?"

"Well, you're oversimplifying, but something like that happens, yes."

"I love you, Del," he said solemnly.

"I love you, too."

"Go on inside," he said when they reached the house, "I'll be in in a minute, okay?"

"Sure."

Del walked into the house that he had helped his mother design when he was little more than a child, the greatest house in the world. He stood in the sand at the bottom of the steps and looked at the ruin of Raymond Sadler's house, then he raised his eyes to the black cloud that still hovered above it, as if reluctant to leave this particular spot on the earth.

"You're a piece of work, Elsbeth," he said softly. Then he climbed the steps to be with his lover and his precious female child, who now had a soul of her own.

THE ONLY ALTERNATIVE IS ANNIHILATION . . .
RICHARD P. HENRICK